HATE YOU

HATE YOU

GRAHAM McNAMEE

DELACORTE PRESS

Published by
Delacorte Press
Random House, Inc.
1540 Broadway
New York, New York 10036

Library of Congress Cataloging-in-Publication Data

McNamee, Graham.
Hate you / Graham McNamee.
p. cm.
Summary: Nursing hatred for the father who choked her and damaged her voice as a child, seventeen-year-old Alice writes songs she feels she cannot sing and seeks to reconcile her feelings for herself and her father.
ISBN 0-385-32593-2
[1. Fathers and daughters—Fiction. 2. Child abuse—Fiction. 3. Singing—Fiction. 4. Self-acceptance—Fiction.] I. Title.
PZ7.M4787934Hat 1999
[Fic]—dc21 98-8047
CIP
AC

The text of this book is set in 12.5-point Adobe Garamond.

Book design by Ericka Meltzer O'Rourke

Manufactured in the United States of America

April 1999

10 9 8 7 6 5 4 3 2 1

BVG

For Stimpy and Fatboy

HATE YOU

Locked in a cell
With my imaginary friends
In a dungeon
Where the night never ends
Every day they slide
Two bowls through the bars
One filled with ashes
The other with tears

And it kills me
That I never got a chance
To tell you
How much
I hate you

I scream for the warden
For the guards for the reason
Why my years have been stolen
For every lost season
I mix ashes with tears
And force it down

My throat turns to stone
And strangles all sound

And I never got a chance
To say how much
I hate you

And I know you can't hear me
Wherever you are
But I'll scream at you anyway
My face to the bars

I hate you
Hate you

—Alice Silvers

CHAPTER 1

That's me, Alice. I write these songs that nobody ever sings. Not even me. See, I have this Frankenstein voice, all cracked, scratched and broken. I can barely get through a sentence without it freaking out on me and frightening dogs and small children. That's me. Even so, I can't stop writing songs.

My favorite color has always been yellow, deep juicy yellow like the color sunlight would be if it were liquid. So that's what I painted my room. Mom says being in here feels like living inside a banana. She also said she read where yellow is the favorite color of insane people. Only she didn't say it like it was funny—Mom sounded like she'd just found a case of condoms, a shopping bag of drugs, a loaded gun and a severed head under my bed. Like she'd found me out. This is how she confronts me with explanations for my own personal weirdness, as if she's figured me out, dug up my forbidden secrets from a shallow grave in the backyard.

She's always reading psych books and true-crime paperbacks, so she sees dementia everywhere. She doesn't worry about normal things, like losing her job or getting raped, she worries about serial killers and flesh-eating diseases and bus hijackers.

And you know what? Just now it came to me, the reason behind Mom's own private weirdness. She's so busy thinking about flesh-eating, bus-hijacking serial killers that she never has a spare moment to think about the real stuff she should be afraid of, like her being forty with zero friends, fleeting romances, sitting around while various body parts sag and wrinkle.

Speaking of wrinkles, here I stand gazing into my shirt drawer. I never mastered the art of folding clothes or the technology of the iron, so I usually look like I've just spent the night curled up in the bottom of my closet, wrinkled as an elephant's butt. Which is fine, "slob chic" is my style.

I choose a lime-green tie-dyed T-shirt. I'm so glad tie-dyeing is out of fashion so I can wear it again. I pull on my white jeans and pull them off. Wearing white jeans at this time of the month is just asking for disaster.

Ever since I went on the Pill, you can set your clock by my blood-flow. I remember the first time I saw Mom's birth control pills I asked her what they were. She said they were vitamins for adults. So after I ate my Flintstones Chewables for the day, I tried one of Mom's vitamins. They tasted terrible! Lucky thing I didn't get hooked on Mom's or I might have hit puberty when I was nine years old.

All I can find in the pile in my closet is a pair of dark brown corduroys. Lime green with brown, plaid sneakers and brown eyes. Will the Fashion Police shoot me on sight?

Downstairs, I find Mom slowly slurping a bowl of Count Chocula in chocolate milk with brown sugar on top. Major sugar junkie! I pour myself a bowl. What can I say? She got me hooked at an early age. Twinkies in the womb. We both have a passion for chocolate. I read where eating it is supposed to ignite the love center of your brain; it's chemistry.

Mom's always saying how she'll only ever marry again if she can find a man with a caramel center and almonds inside. I think she's cracking up—it's all those old hormones creaking along through her system.

We spend five minutes in silence, no hellos or anything. She reads her paper, scanning for murder and chaos. Then she looks up and our eyes meet. Mom's got that look, worried and prepared for shock. When she looks at me like that, it's like she's noticing me for the first time in a long time. I expect her to ask, "Are you still here?" As if I'm supposed to be a memory.

"Are you having sex?" Mom asks, saying that last word like she's just learning the language.

"What? At this moment?" I say.

"No, I mean usually. . . ."

"Yes, Mommie dearest. I'm usually having sex. In fact, I'm late for it right now." I look at my watch and go to get up.

Mom sighs. "I can never talk to you! And don't call me Mommie dearest."

"We can talk. It's just . . . why do you ask a question like that? At breakfast, for God's sake! In the presence of Count Chocula!"

Mom stirs her cereal. "I was just remembering how it was."

"*Sex* isn't dead, Mom. It's still out there."

"It's dead for me. Anyway, I was remembering my first time. . . ."

"Not the ice-fishing story again. I still haven't recovered from hearing it the last time."

A look of irritation crosses Mom's face. I'm supposed to listen. From the dawn of time my role in this family of two was the Listener. I've heard more than I ever wanted to about Mom's life.

"Besides, I'm going to be late," I tell her. "Do I get a ride or do I have to hitch?"

Mom puts the dishes in the sink, then goes to get her shoes. "Don't joke about hitchhiking. That's how Ted Bundy picked up some of those poor girls."

I toss on my army-surplus jacket, the one with all the pockets. I can feel the bulge of my English homework in the inside pocket, untouched. It feels like a time bomb, silently waiting for the report card on Judgment Day.

We pile into the ancient Volkswagen with the remains of the HONK IF YOU'RE A HORNY IRISHMAN bumper sticker—which was half torn off by Mom after she kicked Dad out. Now it just says HONK IF, like it's a philosophical question.

I'm waiting for her to put the keys in the ignition when she starts up again.

"Out on the ice under that black sky, just Raymond and me in that little hut—"

I turn the radio on. Cruel, I know. But still.

"Where's the all-news channel?" I ask. I hate the

news, but it'll make her happy and get me out of hearing that story.

She starts the car. "Ten-fifty AM," she says.

As we putter along in our little crapmobile, I can hear Mom's thoughts as clearly as the newscaster's bland voice. Right now she's adding up the death toll for the day: natural disasters = 36; terrorist attacks = 9; homicides = 2 in the city and 5 more in the Midwest, where another postal worker has cracked under the strain of deciphering cryptic zip codes.

In the backseat, Mom's oversized portfolio case sits on top of a pile of winter clothes. The case shifts as we make a quick right turn. Inside it are Mom's designs for the PlayDead Theater's latest production. She's a set designer, part-time anyway. She paints theatrical backgrounds, landscapes and streetscapes, things to be seen from a distance. That doesn't really pay much, so the rest of the time she works at the City Museum as the art director's assistant, painting all kinds of landscapes in nature dioramas. When you see those lions in their savanna behind glass with all the fake grass and the yellow glow of an imaginary sun, just look past the beasts, the grass and the glow, and you'll see Mom's world in the distance. Far-off mountains capped with snow, high clouds that almost seem to drift on invisibly painted winds, the shadows of other animals grazing out of reach.

When I was about five, I asked Mom to paint Curious George (my childhood soul mate) on my bedroom wall for me. So I got home from kindergarten one day to find George with his monkey feet touching the floorboard as if he was standing there. He was exactly my height. One of his hands was reaching out to a wall socket, with a finger sticking right in the outlet. Curious George's monkey hair, always smooth and neat in the storybooks, was now standing on end in an electric frizz. His eyes were shocked wide. His free hand held a half-peeled banana, which he had squeezed so hard the insides had popped out and were sailing through the air.

I was sure Mom had seen right into my dreams, as if my eyes were clear glass and she peered into them while I slept. It was just so perfect.

I went up to him and touched his arm to see if it was furry like a real monkey's. It felt like a wall, cool and hard. Back then I still dreamed in cartoons, so when I came face-to-face with Curious George it was like walking up to a dream in the light of day. I could feel a sympathetic electric shiver goose-pimpling my skin. I then poured my heart out to the monkey. I told him my greatest secret.

I whispered. "I hate my father."

The monkey didn't blink, didn't make like he heard. But I knew he had.

It couldn't have been much longer after our first meeting—because we were still exactly the same height (I measured)—that my father attacked George with a paint scraper. Dad said the electrified monkey on the wall was gruesome. No, "sick" was the word he shouted at Mom, shouted through the haze of smoke from his cigarette. "Besides," he said. "I just painted this room last year. Now it's ruined."

It's not like he was drunk or anything. He never drank. It would have been easier if he had; then you could explain his behavior away. But no, that was just Dad!

He stabbed at the wall with the scraper until I screamed so loud it left my own ears ringing. I only scared my father twice in my life. That was the first time. He actually backed off a couple steps like I was a threat, still holding the scraper in his fist. Mom was somewhere in the background, silent.

I saved the chipped-off paint, which consisted of George's lower half and most of the arm reaching for the socket. I put it in my book where Curious George learns how to fly a kite with the Man in the Yellow Hat. The rest of the monkey is still on the wall. When I did my room up in yellow, I painted carefully around him. I even stayed clear of the bald patch where the original paint had been stabbed off, just so I would always remember the true story when I looked at my monkey.

George was a survivor, which made us even closer twins of the heart. I told myself George had risked death rather than give up the secret I had shared with him.

CHAPTER 2

When I look at the back of Eric's bald head, I can see a little spot behind his left ear that I missed when I shaved him the other night. Just a bit of blond stubble you wouldn't even notice if you didn't know his head really well. Not to give you the wrong idea, it's not like we indulge in bizarre shaving rituals, nothing so butch. It's just that Eric has this neuromuscular thing with his right hand, so it trembles most of the time—even when he's asleep, which is a truly strange and disturbing thing to discover, believe me. Like someone who sleeps with their eyes open, it makes you nervous in the lonely late-night hours.

The thing of it is, Eric's right-handed—was right-handed. Now he's no-handed. He's had this thing for about six years. It hasn't gotten any worse, but it won't get any better without medication. The pills that stop the shaking leave him nauseous and make him blink rapidly, which drives him nuts.

So his hand shakes. He can scribble-write with his

left, but it turns out like some alien, chicken-scratch language that only he can decipher.

I shave him smooth every other week. I'm always reminded of this TV show I saw once where these Tibetan boys dressed in their best Buddhist robes got their heads shaved clean before they went to live in the monastery. They sat silently as their thick black hair fell to the ground around them. Afterward, they gathered together, laughing as they rubbed each other's bare scalps.

Eric had heavy-metal-Jesus hair down past his shoulders when I first met him two years ago. He was a real idiot back then. Hasn't changed much. He's a master of the insult, and the cutting remark.

The absolute very first time I ever met him he cut me deeply. This was at the beginning of school in September two years ago—probably the second day back in class. Mom had some kind of appointment that morning and I had to get up early so she could drop me off. I was the first one in class, still half asleep. Everything seemed unnaturally bright. I wondered if you could get a fluorescent sunburn from the intense school lighting. Janie, my friend from junior high, arrived and finished putting on her face.

"Have you ever tried putting eyeliner on in a moving car? Almost poked my eye out," she said.

"It's way too early to be conscious," I said. "I'm wearing two pairs of socks, and none of them match. I have no idea why. Can I borrow your mirror?" She was so used to my cracked voice, she didn't notice. Which is great, because I get enough stares from strangers.

Janie handed over the mirror.

I took one look. "Oh, God! Big mistake! I give up." I gave it back.

I was sitting on the teacher's desk, facing the windows and squinting at the late-summer sunlight in the trees. I sighed and lay back on the desk.

"I can't do it. Not another year of this. God, please. Sacrifice me now!"

With my eyes closed I heard a male voice speak from the door to the room.

"I only sacrifice virgins!"

When I sat up and looked around, there stood Eric with his long blond metal hair. He was grinning at the floor. Another guy with him spoke up, shaking his head.

"That's low, Eric."

They went and sat down. I looked at Janie. She rolled her eyes and mouthed the word "Freaks."

That was it, our first meeting. Hate at first sight. The next day he came up to me in the hall and said sorry. "You know, what I said, that didn't mean anything."

"Like I care," I said. And that's all I said to him for a couple of months.

But Eric kept saying sorry every time I ran into him. Even now, Eric's always saying sorry. Sorry for a million things; it's his favorite word.

Anyway, that was the beginning of our tender, torrid love. Freak that he was, I still forgave him.

When he made that idiot remark about sacrificing virgins he had no idea that my virginity had so recently been terminated.

For the past two months of summer vacation before I met Eric, I had been going out with Henry

Sandborn. Don't ask me why. Maybe because he was the first person to ever tell me I was beautiful. Maybe because he didn't get scared when I couldn't stop crying after we did it that first time under the trees in the park on the hottest night of the summer.

I told Henry I loved him. Which is a crazy thing to do, because you can never take it back.

Up close, he was wonderful. As long as he was kissing me, touching me, he was like a dream. But the rest of the time, which was most of the time, he treated me like dirt.

Anyway, he's ancient history. His family moved away. If they hadn't moved, I might have spent another year with Henry. That's a scary thought. I might have missed out on Eric, the love of my life, missed out on our shared destiny and all that garbage.

Back in the classroom, back in real time, Eric touches my shoulder with his shivering hand.

"Al, wake up," he says.

He's looking down at me. I blink up at him. "What?"

"Let's go."

I notice everybody's making a break for the door.

"Class is over?" I ask.

"Yes, dear. Now it's back to the rubber room and the shirts that tie in the back."

I grin. "And the electroshock treatments?"

His grin twins mine. "Only if you're good."

I follow him out.

"To what enchanted land are you taking me now, fair prince?"

"To the cafeteria. Hurry up. We're meeting somebody."

"We are?"

Eric nods. "You know, your pants remind me of a joke."

"Oh, God," I groan. "Okay. Go ahead."

Eric smiles his stupid little smile.

"What's Helen Keller's favorite color?" he asks.

I sigh. "I don't know. What?"

"Corduroy."

I hate his jokes, but I love his stupid little smile.

"You know," I say. "Your face reminds me of a joke."

He laughs and puts his arm around me, hooking his thumb in the belt loop on my hip. I reach up and brush at that bit of blond stubble I missed behind his ear.

CHAPTER 3

Rachel Grant has long ponytailed orange hair, which isn't the first thing you notice about her. The first thing is that she weighs two hundred plus pounds. She dresses all in black. She sits alone.

"So you're Alice," she says when we're introduced. "Eric's told me your whole life story."

I turn to Eric with my eyebrows raised.

"What? What's wrong?" he says. "Don't worry, I left out the good bits."

"There were good bits?" I ask. "I must have missed those."

We sit down side by side facing her.

"Rachel's my cousin," Eric tells me. "We have the same birthday, the same horoscope. We're astrological twins."

"Yeah. And I'm eating for both of us," Rachel says.

Eric fakes a laugh.

How do you react when someone puts themselves down like that? I mean, you can't really burst out laughing or they'll get insulted—even though they've just insulted themselves. Do you smile? Do you say: "No, you're not really that fat." How about an awkward silence?

Rachel swirls her straw around in her Diet Coke. Coming right out with a fat joke is kind of a challenge—like she's saying, don't you dare feel sorry for me.

So I just shake my head and smile a little.

When I spoke a minute ago, my voice only got a small reaction from Rachel. Eric must have warned her not to stare or frown or anything.

"So," Eric says. "Rachel just moved back to town. She was living way out in the middle of nowhere."

"My father's an engineer. They were doing some drilling," Rachel explains. As she talks, she pulls her ponytail so it comes over her shoulder, and runs her fingers over it as if she's petting a cat's tail.

Eric brushes his hand over his bare scalp, like those newly bald Tibetan monk kids. I know every bump on that head. There's nowhere my fingers haven't been.

"I was telling Rachel how you write songs," he says.

I shrug. "Sort of. Yeah." I try to speak low and quiet, but my voice betrays me, jumping in the wrong places.

"Well, Rachel sings. I mean, really sings. Amazingly."

"Oh, right," Rachel says, sounding doubtful. "I'm okay."

"She's lying. She's really amazing. I thought maybe you two could get together, you know?"

Now I clue in. I shake my head. "You probably wouldn't like my stuff," I tell Rachel.

"You might hate my singing."

Eric pokes my shoulder with his index finger until I tell him to quit it.

"I'm not saying you have to sign a recording contract or anything," he says. "You could just try it out. It won't kill you."

Rachel shrugs. "You could come over to my house. We can give it a try."

Well. It won't kill me. Or will it? I've never even thought about someone else singing my songs. Somehow it feels wrong. Like hiring someone else to live your life for you.

Rachel's room looks abandoned; there's nothing on the walls. All she has is a bed, a desk and a chair.

"When do you move in?" I ask.

"This is it," she says. "The whole enchilada. This room is done."

Eric and I look around at the bare white walls.

I have to say it. "It's like—don't take this bad or anything—but it's like a waiting room. A hotel room or something."

Rachel shrugs. "No offense taken. Actually, that's a perfect way to say it. This is a hotel room. We're always moving, because of my dad's job." She crosses her arms over her chest. "Why decorate? I can't take the walls with me."

She walks over and opens the closet door. I notice she's blushing.

"This is where I do my singing. It's weird but the acoustics are really incredible in here."

I peek in. It's a walk-in closet, big enough for the three of us to stand in without feeling like we're hiding from the Nazis. We pile on in. There's a large open trunk in one corner, with clothes folded inside. God, she's not even unpacking. I think I know why she's blushing—she's sort of exposing herself, exposing something even more intimate than her body. This place, this closet, is where her heart is.

"I'm usually alone when I do this," Rachel says, playing with the end of her ponytail.

"Don't worry," Eric tells her. "How about we close the door and leave the light off in here, so it'll be like you're by yourself."

"Let's give it a shot." She nods, and Eric shuts the door, leaving us in blackness with only a thin crack of light from under the door.

"What should I sing?" Rachel's voice comes from the dark.

"How about 'Louie Louie'?" Eric says.

I jab out blindly, my elbow connecting with his ribs. "Shhh," I tell him. "Let me think. Ummm. What was the first song you ever learned?"

"'Amazing Grace'?"

"Sure. Go ahead," I say.

"Okay."

She takes a few seconds, breathing deeply, waking up her lungs.

And she sings.

I would cry right here right now, silently and unseen, except I know I'll have to leave this closet in a minute when this song ends and step back into the light of the real world. This incredible voice, so close it could be coming from inside my own head—this is the voice I dream in. She sings like an angel gave her mouth-to-mouth and left its breath behind in her lungs. This voice is beautiful in every way I can never be.

I'd give up anything to sound like that. Anything. Everything.

I want the last note to stretch out past the length of the longest breath. I want it to last an hour, a day. I imagine it following me out into the world like an echo refusing to die.

Rachel finishes and the quiet takes hold. It feels like walking in a rainstorm, leaning into the wind, and the wind dying so suddenly you're left hanging, unbalanced. As if for a while there the only thing holding you up, the only thing holding you together, was the wind. The song.

"So," Rachel says. "What do you think?"

CHAPTER 4

My father has big hands. One of my earliest, prehistoric memories is of walking beside him along a boardwalk somewhere near the smell of the ocean. Mom was on his other side holding his left hand, while I had his right all to myself, though I couldn't actually hold the whole thing—just one thick finger. It was enough for me. I had to reach up, way up. He looked down and wiggled his finger in my grasp.

"Looks like you caught a little worm there," my father said, squirming his finger in my grip.

That was the funniest thing anyone in the universe had ever said and I giggled like the criminally insane, reaching my other hand up to squeeze the worm.

He was always doing something with his hands, smoking usually. He chain-smoked through my entire childhood, so when I remember him he's lost in a fog, busy filling ashtrays beyond capacity.

My father's hands always seemed close by, so big that I could never really hide from them. I could feel his presence, even if he was in another part of the house, even through closed doors and loud music I felt him the way you feel the electricity when you pass your hand over a television screen. The sort of feeling where your short hairs stand on end, like an invisible touch.

For me, my father *was* his hands—was how they moved, how they touched, what they broke.

My father's hands only ever hurt me once.

Dad was never a hitter or a slapper. I don't think he liked the sound of it. He didn't like loud noises at all. I discovered that the day he attacked Curious George with the paint scraper. My scream went through him like acoustic lightning, scared him so bad he flinched and took a step back as if this little kid with the wailing lungs was a threat. As if I could hurt him.

Dad wasn't a hitter—he was a squeezer, a grabber and a shaker. He left five-fingered bruises on Mom's wrists, biceps, shoulders and neck—and maybe other places I never saw.

He didn't squeeze or grab or shake me, though. He made me laugh until I couldn't breathe. Dad was a sadistic tickler, poking my ribs and under my arms, leaving me dizzy and numb. I would shout at him to stop, and he would smile back at me. "Can't take it, eh? Can't take it?" He would smile, and even now I don't think he meant to hurt me or anything. This was just his version of the fatherly pat on the head, the only way he could be physical with me. Being afraid and laughing at the same time is the strangest feeling in the world. It's as if your body is possessed, out of your control. You can only watch it from a distance. It took me the longest time after Dad was gone forever to learn how to really laugh again, to trust that laugh as my own, and not feel the electric shiver of those hands closing in on me.

I only ever scared my father twice. The second time was the last time I ever saw him.

It went like this.

When they fought, I always wished Mom would just shut up. What was she thinking, yelling back at him like that? Had she forgotten what happened the last time she shouted back?

That night we were all in the living room. I was eating a bag of Chee-tos, carefully licking my orange-tipped fingers after each one. There was a movie on TV about alien abductions, where the aliens basically took you away and gave you a physical. I wondered where I could apply to be abducted. When I was small, I always liked going to the doctor's. There was tons of stuff to look at and I could steal a few things when the doctor left the room. Just little things. Nothing serious. Latex gloves, or gauze (which came in handy for mummifying my dolls when I got home), or the occasional thermometer. But in the movie they wrapped the abductee in plastic wrap, like he was a sandwich, which I decided wouldn't be so much fun.

Mom and Dad were arguing, first in the kitchen, then in the living room. I have no idea what it was about. I was trying to block out the frequencies of their voices, the way I saw the FBI do in this movie where they had to filter all the distorting sounds from a recording to hear the serial killer's confession. But the FBI had a supercomputer and all I had was a ten-year-old brain.

They were getting louder. Not a good sign.

I tried to be totally silent. I made sure I didn't crinkle the bag in my lap and I let the Chee-tos dissolve in my mouth instead of crunching them. Using the TV remote, I turned the volume down so I couldn't hear the creepy alien music playing in the background as the abductee woke up on the mother ship.

To this day I can't remember what they were shouting at each other. I just know I could feel their words in my chest as if they had a physical force, the same way deep bass chords can vibrate your bones when you stand in front of speakers.

I focused on the TV screen and tried to lose myself there. I wished I had blinders like those street horses downtown. But out of the corner of my eye I saw Dad grab her. She instantly shut up. There was a second of silence, the kind of quiet something makes falling from a great height.

My head turned by itself. I couldn't look away from them.

He had her wrist in his hand, white knuckles squeezing her. Every muscle in her face was clenched, eyes bright and wet. I could tell she was holding back a whimper. He shouted in her face, his mouth close enough to kiss her. Mom's eyes shut tight.

His hands moved to her throat. Mom's throat was thin enough for one of his hands to wrap nearly all the way around. Her arms hung limp, as if she was paralyzed—like a kitten grabbed by the scruff of its neck.

White knuckles squeezing.

I was standing before I knew I'd moved. My bare feet stepped on Chee-tos, mashing them into the rug. I was possessed, like when he tickled me past exhaustion into numbness and I kept on laughing. I watched my hand as if I was looking the wrong way through a telescope, as if it was a thousand miles away. I watched my hand reach up and touch his hot, bare arm.

"Stop," I said. It was the last word I ever said with my real voice, my unbroken voice. (I can almost hear the sound of it now, if I sit really still in the dark.)

He dropped Mom and her legs crumpled. She hit the floor.

His eyes were blind when they turned on me. He wasn't seeing me. Those big hands closed in, smelling of Camel smoke and the perfume Mom rubbed behind her ears. He lifted me off the floor by my neck without even straining, holding me so close my nose bumped off his cheek. I held on to his wrists, leaving orange cheese-powder smudges. My vision blurred into static, into black.

I woke up on the back porch in the cold night air.

"Baby. Baby. Baby," someone was saying in a voice thick with tears. "Baby. Baby."

I opened my eyes slowly. Even the pale wash of light from the house was too bright. I had to squint against the pain the brightness made behind my eyes.

"Baby. Baby."

Someone held me in their arms, someone with small warm hands.

"Baby."

My throat burned. It felt like I was breathing through the thinnest of straws. I reached up to my throat and stabs of pain flared up at my touch.

"Baby. Alice. It's over. It's over. He's gone now," Mom was saying. "Over. All over."

Two days later, Dad called. Mom had just gotten home with takeout when the phone started ringing. I grabbed my two chocolate milk shakes from the bag—that's about all I ate for a couple of weeks. Soup and milk shakes and sundaes (no nuts, no sprinkles).

I stopped stirring the shake when I heard Mom's voice drop. I could see her standing in the kitchen. Her voice was low and steady but I saw her legs were shivering. It was contagious. My stirring hand started shaking too, just a little, like it was possessed.

I couldn't make out any words until she said:

"It's dead. The whole thing is just dead."

Silence while she listened for a second.

"No. No. I took her to the hospital. They took Polaroids. You ever come here again and the police will put your sick ass in jail."

A pause.

"That's crap. You can see your whole handprint on her neck, like a tattoo."

A longer silence.

"That's right. Never again. Never."

Mom took the phone away from her ear. Her shoulders slouched forward and she rocked gently, breathing like she'd just run a sprint. She set the receiver down.

The truth was, I never went to the hospital. Mom was afraid they would take me away if they found out. She did take a Polaroid. She was thinking like a detective in one of her true-crime books. Collecting evidence. Mom pulled me from school, which was fine by me. I wore a turtleneck all through the spring, as if I was hiding a hickey.

In September I switched schools. Nobody knew me

in the new place, so no one realized that my voice was a recent devastation. They just thought I was a born freak, no explanation necessary.

My voice never came back, not my real voice anyway. What you hear now is a broken record, scratched to hell. Mom and Eric say I don't sound so bad, but they don't have to hear it from the inside.

One last thing before I shut up.

Mom's got a big mouth. The part of the brain that censors what you say is totally missing in her. It's like a genetic mutation, like being color-blind. If she thinks something, she says it out loud.

How many times have I thought to myself: "Wow! I really didn't need to know that."

For example, the touching story of how Mom lost her cherry in an ice-fishing hut.

Here's another. The funny thing about this one is that she didn't even have to say anything. Everything was communicated in a gesture.

Me and Mom were sitting on the couch in the living room, about a week after Dad was permanently exiled. An ancient rerun of *M*A*S*H* was on and I was trying to laugh silently so I wouldn't tear up my throat. I was on the ice-cream diet. The cool felt great running down inside. Mom was eating potato chips, which smelled great but would feel like razor blades if I tried to swallow one.

The show faded into commercials. I glanced over at Mom. She was staring into space, running her fingertips along the soft skin of her throat, slowly, as if she was tracing every ridge and delicate bone of her windpipe.

Then it suddenly flashed on me, how many times

had I seen his hands on her throat? From playful touches to enraged, red-faced strangling. The night I got in his way wasn't the first time he'd done that to Mom. I realized then that it had happened before, times I never saw. Behind closed doors.

I ran and made it to the bathroom before I puked up everything I'd ever eaten.

I'd seen five-fingered bruises on her before, seen him brush his fingers over the pale skin of her neck, seen her try to mirror his smile when he touched her there. That was the worst thing though, how gentle he could be, like petting a dog before he whipped it.

Now he's vanished, fallen off the ends of the earth. After a quick divorce he wasn't even my father anymore—at least that's how Mom explained it to me back then. No alimony or anything. Mom called it blood money, and said we'd never be rid of him if we took it.

If they could find the part of my brain where the memory of my father is stored, I would gladly let the surgeons slice it out. Even if I had to lose some other stuff too, like calculus or Fat Elvis or the Spice Girls. But I read somewhere that memories get stored all over the place in triplicate and quintuplicate. They can spread like a killer disease.

CHAPTER 5

Lying on my bed, staring at my banana ceiling, I listen to an angel. A large, orange-haired angel who dresses in black for invisibility. Only I can hear her, tangled in the headphone cord that wraps around me like an anorexic boa constrictor.

Rachel is singing my "Hate You" song. If I unfocus my ears a little, so I just hear the sound of the words but not their meaning, it sounds like a love song. Sad, warm, with a touch of longing and loss. So beautiful you want to cry and fall in love at the same time—which could get kind of messy.

It's like a few years ago when all I listened to was Enya, and I never really focused on the words so much as the feel of the music. It's the kind of music you hear in psychedelic dream elevators. If I listen hypnotically tranced like that, Rachel's singing hits me like a shot of honeyed adrenaline straight to the heart.

But if I really hear the words, what they mean and how they burn, then Rachel's "Hate You" sounds like a lie.

Hate's supposed to burn, supposed to tear and shatter. And hurt. You don't have to be a brain surgeon to see that Rachel's saving up all her hate for herself, aiming it all at that beating red muscle in her chest.

I don't think I'll ever do or be anything as beautiful as the sound of Rachel's voice. Somewhere in the dusty corners of my mind I hate her for that. A weird kind of hate that reminds me of the taste of cigarette ash in warm Coke, a taste that goes right through you, that you never forget. I feel stupid for feeling this way.

I feel even stupider that I still daydream how if Dad hadn't squeezed my throat to dry pulp, maybe I could have had Rachel's angel-honeyed voice. Been beautiful.

That dream feels stale; ash in warm Coke.

YOU'LL NEVER KNOW HER

You found her in your sleep, in your screams
In the amazing wreckage of your dreams
You carried her to safety
To the shade beneath the trees
And sent a prayer to heaven
Fell down onto your knees
You said if she'd stay with you awhile
You'd write her name across the miles

But the clocks have all stopped moving
Each insect wheel and arm
And the sands of time have blown away
Blinding others with their charm
You scream at all who'll hear you
How such beauty came to harm

And you'll never know her laughter
Her voice her touch her lips
As she falls apart before you
Beneath your fingertips
Never know, you'll never know
Never never know her

Her skin peels away in pages
Of tiny printed words
That scatter on the wind like flocks
Of tiny printed birds
The pages come too fast
You lose them to the wind
Catching words like love and heat
And dreams coming to an end

And you'll never know never know
Never never know her
Never know what you lost
And never ever hold her

CHAPTER 6

I'm glad Rachel's fat. There, I said it.

That's been swimming around in my head for weeks now, like a turd floating in a public pool. Such an ugly thought. Here she is, this honey-voiced, kind, shy girl, and I'm glad that in some way she's not perfect.

There was this thing on the news a few years ago about a failed artist who attacked Michelangelo's *David*—you know, the statue of the naked guy with the wavy hair and the little weenie—attacked it with a hammer. This loser who couldn't cut it in the big leagues of the art world tried to take down a thing of perfect beauty. All because he couldn't make it, didn't have the magic in him.

I feel like that loser. Here I am, banging garbage can lids together hoping to drown out an angel.

There was this other guy on the news—the news is all Mom ever watches (besides *Cops* and *America's Most Wanted*). Another unknown artist wannabe, this man goes around to galleries in New York and vomits on paintings he thinks are bad. He's making a STATEMENT.

I don't want to be like these losers. Ugly inside.

I don't want to hate Rachel, or tear her down.

But I have to stay clear of her for now, or else I'll hurt her.

CHAPTER 7

So where do I end up the very next day? At the movies with Eric and Rachel.

Last class of the day I had twentieth-century American history; Rachel and Eric had chemistry. So when I met them at my locker, they'd already decided on a movie. I couldn't say no. Then Rachel would know it was because of her.

I guess I can survive sitting two hours in the dark, with Eric between us. Besides, it'll be good to watch a flick and put my brain on autopilot.

"What's this thing called again?" I ask Eric as he steals a fistful of popcorn from me.

"*Dying in Your Dreams.*"

"Oh good, a comedy," I say.

"It's supposed to be a science-fiction-film-noir kind of thing. Like *Blade Runner,* but not so upbeat."

I groan. "I think I'm going to need some serious chocolate to get through this."

Rachel leans over Eric. "Here, hold out your hand," she says, pouring me a palmful of M&M's.

"Thanks. Hey, you guys were just in chemistry. I read how chocolate has this chemical that stimulates the love center of the brain."

"Great," Eric says. "I think I'll pour some down my pants."

"Well, that is the location of *your* brain," I tell him.

Eric grins like an idiot. Me and Rachel just shake our heads in disgust.

"Seriously though, that's true," Rachel says. "I forget what the chemical's called, but even the smell of chocolate can do it for you. Make you feel all warm inside."

I laugh with her.

The lights go down. I chew my M&M's slowly, sucking all the love out of them.

On the bus home we talk movie soundtracks. Eric loved the music in *Dying in Your Dreams.* It was really harsh and grating—lots of industrial noise, cymbal crashes, electric squeals—reflecting the nightmare futureworld in the movie.

"It was like the scoring in that movie *Seven.* You know, the serial-killer movie with Brad Pitt. It's like how a migraine would sound put to music," Eric says.

Rachel brushes the tip of her ponytail on the underside of her chin. "There was that one beautiful piece of music that followed the woman on the run through the picture. The soprano piece. I think it's from an opera."

"I know," I say. "That was amazing. Really haunting, you know. God, to have that voice. So pure it could shatter glass." I look over at Rachel. "You have a voice like that."

She blushes and stares at her feet. "The only thing I shatter is mirrors."

Eric punches her in the arm a couple times. "You gotta stop that."

Rachel shrugs him off and gives me a sideways look. "I'd like to hear you sometime. I mean, hear how you'd sing your songs. Your way."

"Oh, right. My way. Then you'd know the meaning of pain. My singing could shatter concrete. Make deaf men weep."

Eric gives me a few shots in the arm. "Stop. Stop. Stop. You guys." He shakes his head.

"You hear what I sound like now, talking in a normal tone. I sing and it just gets worse. The louder it gets, the more I lose control. You're the soprano. I'm industrial noise. And stop punching me," I say, shoving Eric. "It's true."

Rachel gets off a few stops before me. Eric's stop is another ten blocks farther on. When we're alone, he puts his arm around me and I lean into him.

"Could you do something?" he asks. "I mean, do it for me?"

"What's that?"

He curls my hair around his finger, lets it unravel and curls it again.

"Hang out with Rachel. She could . . . You could be good for her. She's important."

"Important?"

"To me," he says. "We've always been close. Even when she was way off somewhere, we always wrote."

"I . . ." I'm about to say *I don't know,* but I stop myself. "I . . . could do that."

"You'd be good for her. Maybe she'd be good for you, too."

I take in one last deep breath of him. "My stop's coming up. Kiss me good night."

"Good night."

CHAPTER 8

The backseat of our tiny car is packed to the roof with paint cans, brushes, rollers and a portfolio case big enough to fit a four-by-five-foot saltine cracker (the kind they used to feed the extras when they filmed *The Birds*).

Instead of a cracker, though, the case contains Mom's stage designs for the latest production of the PlayDead Theater Company. I had to pick up her order from the art-supplies store because she's busy mind-melding with the director over his vision for the play.

She gets paid less than zero for all the work she puts into these productions. She's doing what she loves, though, I guess. Starving for her art and all that.

I park by the back door. The door's wide open. They're still trying to air the place out after their last production. I can smell chlorine in the air, a smell that triggers a million memories of swimming lessons, diving for pennies, coughing up gallons of bright blue water and the sound of voices echoing under the mile-high ceilings of indoor pools.

I grab Mom's portfolio from the backseat and take it inside. As I walk down the dim hallway past the dressing rooms, the smell gets stronger.

The last production closed a week ago after a two-month run. Mom said it actually made a profit, even after you factored in the water damage to the stage.

The play was called *Big City Lifeboat.* I was there opening night. If I don't show up to see Mom's stage designs in action on the first night, she gets all quiet and depressed for days. Like I stood her up on a date or something.

The *Lifeboat* play took place entirely in one of those big round portable pools. They had the stage lowered so the audience could look down at the actors, floating in a dinghy on the chlorinated water. The whole idea is that this married couple goes for a late-night skinny-dip in their backyard pool, only to discover when they're finished frolicking that they're lost. They can't find their way back to the side of the pool. The rest of the play is spent with the couple whining about how alone they feel, deserted by society, shipwrecked from the rest of the world.

Believe it or not, *Big City Lifeboat* got great reviews. "A tale of modern alienation," one newspaper column read. "An examination of the urban heart," said another.

"The longest hour and a half of my life," is what I say. The reason the production made a profit was due mainly to the fact that the actors were stark naked for the whole thing. A postmodern, existential nudie show.

Climbing the stairs to the backstage, I can hear Elvis singing from a radio that he can't help falling in love with me. His voice is fractured by the pounding of flooring hammers. If I was Elvis, I would definitely leave the building.

Two guys are fixing the hardwood stage floors. I make a detour around them.

Mom is sitting with a man at a table in the pit by the front of the stage. Piles of open books are arranged on the table with bits of Kleenex marking off pages of interest.

"Alice." Mom spots me lugging her portfolio case. "Oh, wonderful. Did you pick up the order?"

"It's all out in the car," I say, leaning the case against the wall.

Mom's wearing a ton of makeup. Something's happening here. She usually goes out plain faced, or with just a hint of eyeliner. But here is the full treatment, the whole K mart ten-minute makeover.

"This is Andrew Warner," she introduces the guy beside her. "He's from the Art Institute."

"Hi. I'm just really only a film student," he says, shaking his head.

He looks like he's about twenty, with cold eyes and a little goatee he's working on to cover a chin that's missing in action. You never realize how important a chin is until it's not there. I see how close to him Mom's sitting, practically lap-dancing, and I feel the heat rising in my cheeks. God, how can she do that? It's so pathetic. Middle-aged woman rubbing up against a guy barely past acne—like something from a Tennessee Williams play.

I check the time, fiddle with my watch. "So, do you want me to unload the supplies?"

"Yes," Mom says, touching this Warner guy's forearm. "We'll help out. Andrew?"

"Oh, of course," he says.

I lead the way out back so I don't have to watch them. I hurry and carry as much as I can so as not to prolong the agony.

There's something about this Warner I don't like. "You don't like anybody," I can practically hear Eric in my head saying. "You hate everything." And I'll admit, I can be a sour old hag. But there's this way Warner stares at me, his bright blue eyes like frozen chlorine. You could skate on those eyes.

When me and Mom are out by the car together, alone for the moment, I ask her why she needs a film student.

"For the new play. You know, *Last Train Leaving*—I've only been talking about it for the last month."

I shrug. "Right, the train thing. So where does film come into it?"

We grab paint cans from the trunk.

"Well, remember the lead character is taking this final train trip home. She's dying, and—"

"Dying from what?" I ask.

"I don't know. They don't say. Doesn't matter." Mom sounds mildly annoyed.

"It would matter to me."

"She's terminally ill," Mom tells me.

"That's a little vague. Maybe she should get a second opinion." I'm being annoying on purpose.

She makes a major effort to ignore me. "The whole

play takes place in a passenger compartment. So we're just using the center of the stage, front and center, close to the audience. The rest of the stage will be blocked off with white curtains." I follow Mom up the stairs. Elvis is calling out that he wants to be my teddy bear. The flooring guys give him no mercy, cracking his words into tiny pieces.

Mom goes on. "When she's alone in the scene, we're going to project film of steam-engine trains across the whole stage, over the curtains, the actress and everything. It's going to look amazing."

Sometimes her ideas aren't too bad. "When's the play open?"

"In three weeks. Plenty of time. The whole stage design is basically the one compartment. A bench, a door, a window."

"Where you getting the projection equipment from?"

"That's where Andy comes in," she tells me.

Andy? Andy!

"Andy needs to do a practicum for his finals. I'm his practicum."

"His practicum? Sounds kinky," and I sneer to show her I'm kidding.

Mom just shakes her head. "Where did you come from anyway?"

"I think the stork must've been wasted that night and had to crash at your place."

Mom sighs a long gusty one. "I didn't hear that. Anyway, a practicum is when you do a project in the real world, not just in a class somewhere. I talked to the people at the Art Institute and they sent me Andy. He's free, and we get free use of the projectors."

We set the last load down by the stage-side table. Warner is stacking his books to make room for the portfolio case. Mom puts a hand on his shoulder, saying, "Andy gets graded on how well he pulls this off."

He smiles. "My entire cinematic future is in your hands."

They start spreading the designs out on the table. "So," I say. "Should I take the Beetle or the bus?"

"Oh, you take it, Alley. Andy's got a car. He'll give me a lift." She turns to him with raised eyebrows. Obviously, she hasn't asked him yet.

"Sure," he says. "No problem."

What a shameless tart. I meet his eyes for a second. They're still cold, but they seem nervous now, sensing the widow's web he's stumbled into closing in around him.

As I leave I hear that Elvis has gotten over falling in love with me, and he no longer wants to be my teddy bear. Now he's telling Mom that it's all right. That's all right, Momma.

And I guess it is, all right I mean. All right to chase whoever you want. I think I just have this toxic reaction to testosterone. Warner seems harmless. Mom, on the other hand, I'm not so sure about.

CHAPTER 9

The phone is ringing when I get home from the theater. We have this call-display thingy that tells you who's calling, so you can avoid talking to relatives and loan sharks. I run and check the display.

UNKNOWN. Unknown means long distance.

Should I? Shouldn't I? My hand hovers over the receiver. Another ring.

"Hello," I say.

"Oh, hi." The voice on the other end sounds surprised. A woman's voice. There's a long pause and I wonder if I've been cut off. Then she's back. "Sorry. I just— I've been letting it ring about a hundred times. Didn't think anyone would answer."

"I usually give up after fifty rings myself," I say. "Wouldn't want to seem obsessive, you know?"

There's a small quiet laugh on the other end. "I sound crazy. Let me start over. I'm calling for someone named Alice Silvers?"

I shrug out of my jacket and sit down on the couch, wondering what kind of trouble I'm in.

"That's me."

"Oh, good. Um, you don't know me. Obviously. My name is Linda Rossetti. And . . . I'm sort of your father's girlfriend."

I hold the phone away from my face and stare at it like it just stung me. Everything seems totally strange and alien—the coffee table, the TV, the Bahamas poster on the wall—all from a stranger's house on a stranger's planet. My father? I want to say, "I don't have a father." But I can't. I stare at the receiver and my hand holding it. I painted my fingernails last week in a shade called Drop Dead Red, and I see how it's chipped away. It looks awful. I remember the nail polish, and then the coffee table, the TV, the beach by the blue Caribbean on the wall. I remember everything.

"Still there?" Linda Rossetti's voice sounds thin and small with the phone in my lap. I bring it to my ear.

"Still here," I say.

"I wouldn't call—I wouldn't bother you. It's just that your father . . . He's in the hospital."

There's this long silence. Is she waiting for me to say something? What am I supposed to say?

"The hospital," she repeats. "Oh God. This is hard. Your father. In the hospital. And he's dying. Dying."

That strange alien feeling comes over me again like a sudden vertigo. If I'm not careful I could fall a long, long way. With the thumbnail of my free hand I chip at the old red polish. It's like this one small action pulls me back to reality.

"Dying." I echo the word before I think it, like it's bouncing off me.

"Yes."

"Why?" I ask, but it's the wrong question. "I mean how? What's he dying from?"

"Cancer." She whispers the word as if cancer is close by on her end, wherever she is, and might hear her speaking about it.

A big piece of Drop-Dead Red chips off and falls on the carpet, looking like a drop of blood.

"Lung cancer," I say.

"Yes."

Some deep part of my brain must be freaking out on me, because for a second I can smell cigarette smoke, only it has the heavy, dusty taste of old smoke, stained into the furniture, the drapes, the carpet. Camels. He always smoked Camels. Said if you were going to use coffin nails, they might as well be the best.

The thought comes to me: There's something wrong here. I mean, everything's wrong here! But there's one particular thing that's bugging me. An itch I can't reach.

"Why did you call?" I ask. "I mean, how did you get the number? What made you think to call?"

"Well, Frank, your father, he asked for you. Wanted me to let you know."

Why? Why! It was a question I couldn't really ask her. I was just a name to her, a voice in the distance.

"Did he want to speak to my mother?"

"I don't know. He just said you."

"I don't know what to say."

"Yeah, I know. I really didn't want to make this call. It's been killing me all day. Then I finally do it and I just let it ring and ring, and I couldn't hang up. Oh God. Listen to me, what an idiot. He's your father, and here I am losing it. I'm sorry."

"No. No," I say. God, how do I get out of this? How do I end this? "Um, well, what hospital is he at?"

"St. Paul's."

"What city is that in?" It must sound weird to not know what city your father is living in, is dying in. But what do I care how it sounds?

This Linda Rossetti tells me the city. It's only two hours away. All these years he was so close, a bus ride away. I'd never really thought about where he'd ended up. He disappeared, that's all I knew. And he wasn't coming back. I felt a small shiver run up my neck, knowing he'd been so close.

She gives me her number. I scribble all these names and numbers on the back of my hand with a pen.

And then there's nothing left to say.

"So," she says. "Are you going to come see him, do you think?"

That question is like a stone dropped in a bottomless pit. Nothing comes back, not even an echo.

"I don't . . . I don't know," is all I can manage.

"Oh—never—never mind. I shouldn't ask. I always talk before I think. It's just, he'd really like it if you came. I can tell. That's all."

"That's *all*? That's ALL?" Suddenly I am shouting into the phone. "He'd *like* it? Are you *crazy*? Don't you know—" I stop. We listen to each other's breathing.

"I'm—I'm really sorry," she says.

"Whatever," I say. I don't care.

"So you have my number."

"Yes."

"Okay. Well, bye, then."

"Yes. Bye."

My hands are all sweaty. The phone is slippery in

my grip as I set it down. I imagine a kind of fever-sweat that would sweep over me, making me sweat so hard it would wash the ink from the back of my hand. Erase the words and numbers. Wash away the last few minutes.

But there's still that piece of bloodred polish on the carpet to remind me.

CHAPTER 10

Mom and Eric met by accident. She was supposed to be at work. I was supposed to be at school.

It was the middle of the afternoon, a rainy day last spring. We were cutting the last two classes of the day. Me and Eric were tangled on the couch. The TV was on but nobody was watching. I was exploring Eric's ear with my tongue when I heard the key in the door. Jumping up, I clipped his chin with my shoulder. He muffled a yelp as he bit down on his tongue.

I made sure all zippers were zipped and hit the unmute button on the remote. The room was flooded with "Can you tell me how to get, how to get to Sesame Street?"

Mom's head poked around the corner.

"Oh," she said. "You're home? What . . ." Then she caught sight of Eric. "Oh."

I shrugged. "I was feeling sick. So . . ."

She was staring at Eric.

"He's sick too," I told her.

Eric gave a little wave. "Hi. I'm Eric."

Mom smiled. "I've heard so little about you. I'm Desiree. The mother." She gave me the eye. "I'm the one who gets all those nice little notes from the principal when her daughter doesn't show up for class. Notes and phone calls."

I shrugged again. "It's just the last couple of classes today. Nothing major."

She was still giving me the eye.

"And it won't happen again," I said.

She nodded. "And it definitely won't happen again."

There was an endless silence.

"You guys hungry?" Mom asked.

I headed off disaster by making sure Mom didn't cook. We ordered Chinese.

Mom had been bugging me to bring Eric over for months. I'd been putting it off. I wanted to keep them separate, two different universes. It hurt Mom's feelings, but sometimes it seems it's impossible not to. Her feelings are so large, they take up the whole room, and they're all marked FRAGILE. Nothing less than a total mind-meld would really satisfy her.

But now Mom and Eric were actually talking. I felt dazed. Confused.

"Alice told me you do some of the dioramas at the museum."

"Just the backgrounds, the back walls," Mom said.

"How about the one with the cheetah?"

"That's an old one. I did that ages ago."

"It's my favorite. Since I was a kid. The way the cheetah's just about to jump on the gazelle and take it down."

Mom blushed just a tiny bit, so you probably

wouldn't even notice if you didn't see her every day. "You go there a lot?"

"Yeah. Just for the animals, though. I can't get into armor and tapestries and stuff."

I thought Eric would go into convulsions if he met Mom, but here it's me with the rapid heartbeat.

"Next time you go, check out the clouds and the trees in the background. I tried to whip up the clouds, stretch them out as if they're caught up in the chase with the cheetah. And the trees are bent just a bit, kind of windswept. Adds to the effect."

Eric nodded. "I'll look for that."

Mom nodded back and they smiled.

When the Chinese food came, I got a second alone with Eric.

"You okay?" he asked me. "You're kind of quiet."

"Yes. No. This is just too weird."

Eric shrugged. "She's got your eyebrows."

"What?" I reached up and rubbed them, as if checking to make sure they were still there.

"Little help here?" Mom said, wrestling two big bags into the kitchen.

We tore them open. I grabbed forks and spoons. When I turned around, I caught Mom watching Eric. He was bent over, emptying the bags, and she was looking at his newly shaven head. It was shiny in the kitchen light and I could see a little smudge of my shade of lipstick on the crown. Mom's eyes shifted to meet mine.

There was this look in them I still haven't been able to figure out. There was something sad there, as if she'd just lost something or was just about to. And when she looked at me that way, I felt weak somehow. I can't explain.

"I'm starving," Eric said, peeling the lid off a container of wonton soup.

"Me too," I said.

And we all ate like hogs.

CHAPTER 11

There used to be a kind of pseudoscience called phrenology, the study of the shapes and contours of a person's skull to find out how smart someone's going to be, or what kind of personality they'll have. (Thank you, Mr. Blair from social studies, I actually remember something from your class.)

They used to diagnose you as a genius, a criminal or a psychotic based on the shape of your head. Saves you a lot of time knowing you're destined to be a loser, an Einstein or just criminally insane.

I'm thinking this as I run my fingers over Eric's stubbly head. Who are you really? I ask him silently. What are you becoming? Is it all here under my fingers, beneath this blond peach fuzz?

People should wear little name tags that tell you what they are. Like this:

Lucy. Destiny: Classical Pianist
Personality: Cold but Harmless

Or maybe this:

Jake. Destiny: Professional Wrestler
Personality: Mean and Abusive

It would make everything so much easier. You say hi, read their tag and make your choice.

Eric's head moves in my lap. We trashed school today at my suggestion. I couldn't face another day of calculus brainwashing and chemical bonding. Now we're on the couch at Eric's place. *Oprah*'s muted on the TV. Outside you can smell wood smoke in the air from fireplaces ending their summer hibernation. All the trees are balding, and children everywhere are being buried in fallen leaves.

"Let's go out," I say.

"Where?"

"Anywhere."

Eric looks up at me. "But we've got the place all to ourselves. We can do the forbidden dance." He waggles his eyebrows suggestively.

"I forgot my tap shoes."

"No shoes necessary. Actually, you don't have to wear anything. You can keep your socks on, though."

He's always bugging me about wearing socks in bed. My feet get cold easy.

Eric's right hand disappears up my shirt.

"Where do you think you're going?" I say.

"Exploring."

His hand is so warm on my breast, even the constant trembling feels good. I try to shrug him off. I don't want to feel good right now. "Quit it."

"Why?"

"Get your gimpy hand off me, Romeo."

His hand slides away. He sighs. One thing I've learned in my two years with Eric—teenage guys walk around with permanent erections. Let me modify that—if they're not in the process of having an erection, they're on the verge of having one, they've just had one and are considering another, or they're spending quality time with their erection. They wake up with one every morning and go to sleep after one every night.

Poor Eric.

"What's wrong?" he asks.

I look down into his brown eyes. "Why does something have to be wrong if I don't feel like groping and grunting?"

"Come on. You've been pissed off since I picked you up this morning. Wait, is it the Curse? Your monthly visitor?"

I knock on his forehead. "Anybody home in there? My curse ended a week ago. What, do I have bionic ovaries?"

"Sorry, I forgot to mark it on my calendar."

Eric sits up and grabs the converter to unmute *Oprah.*

"I got a phone call last night," I tell him.

"Okay . . ."

"It's my, um, father. He's dying." My voice shakes even more than normal. I bite my lip.

There's a long silence. Then Eric speaks. "Wow."

Eric's not good at serious moments of the nonsexual variety. He freezes up and plays dead, as if any sound or sudden move might be dangerous, might alert the predator in the room—which in this case would be me.

"What, um . . . How do you feel about that?" he asks after a lot of mental deliberation.

"I don't know. It's there."

"It's there," he says. It's always safe to repeat. That's what psychologists are supposed to do, ask you questions and then repeat what you say so you hear your own answer coming back at you.

"I mean, he's out there. Alive. Well, barely. It's just, I always thought he was gone forever. I thought that part of my life was over. He's been dead to me for like seven years already. Since he left."

The thing about Eric, even when he wants to stay all silent and still, his right hand shivers, a dead giveaway. "Kind of like those nightmares where you wake up and think you've escaped, but you're still trapped in the dream."

He reduces all my feelings to a cliché. My first reaction is to tear into him, tell him he's an idiot. But I stop myself. I don't hate him. Not Eric. He's not the one.

"So how do you end a nightmare?" I ask him.

"I guess you can wait it out, keep running as fast as you can. Or you can stand your ground and take your chances."

CHAPTER 12

Sitting at my desk in my room, I invade North Korea with Janis Joplin. The song "Piece of My Heart" is screaming in my ears, with Janis sounding insane with emotion, eaten alive by it. She always looked to me like a bag lady. Tangled greasy hair, bewildered expression, goofy smile, her brain nuked by pharmaceuticals and alcohol. The combination of her bleeding vocals and the endless chapter on the Korean War I'm reading is sending my brain into a meltdown.

I used to hate her stuff. Her singing really got under my skin, like one of those splinters that won't surface. She had no right to sing. Her voice wasn't crippled like mine, but it definitely had that ugly jagged edge. Eric's into Hendrix, Joplin and Morrison, all those ancient burnouts. Listening to Janis was like cleaning my ears out with steel-wool Q-Tips. Eric forced me to listen.

It took a while, but it grew on me. Now it's like her voice gets to that itch I've never been able to reach. Not that it feels good, so much as it feels right. Feels true.

The pounding of drums changes to pounding on my door. I hit the stop button on the CD player. Silence descends like a concrete pillow.

"What?"

"It's me." Mom opens the door. In one hand she's holding a paperback open, in the other a half-eaten Oh Henry! bar.

"You just get home?" I ask.

"Little while ago. I was reading in the kitchen." She peels the wrapper like a banana and takes another bite of the chocolate bar. "Did you know John Wayne Gacy murdered thirty-three young men and buried them in the crawl space under his house? I think he's the biggest serial killer ever. He was put to death in ninety-four. The electric chair." She pauses to swallow and shake her head. "So many horrible people out there doing horrible things."

I miss Janis's screaming. "You're just a ray of sunshine, aren't you?" I say.

"It just makes me sick." Mom shakes her head.

"Not too sick to stop eating. Anyway, how was your date?"

"I wouldn't call it a date. We talked about the play, about movies and stage design. Nothing romantic really." She flattens out the wrapper and licks her fingers.

I stretch and yawn big-time. "So I won't have to hose out the backseat of the Beetle?"

She frowns and ignores me.

"Andrew's so young. And I'm so old." Mom walks over to my window and peeks around the curtain as if there might be a serial murderer hiding in the trees.

"Are you having cradle-robbing remorse?"

She laughs. "Not remorse. Just doubts. What do you think of him?"

"I think he's a dreamboat. Come on, I don't know." I yawn again, but Mom is actively ignoring the hint. "He's got cold eyes."

"People always say blue eyes are cold, but when you look into them—it's like the sky, it never ends, you can lose yourself, get lost in them."

I kill the smile that's forming on my lips, but I can't help saying something. "Have you been reading those romance novels again? Call Missing Persons, she's lost in someone's eyes again. If you lose your heart, I know where we can get one cheap on the black market. Of course, there's some assembly required."

Mother sighs theatrically. "So young to be so jaded. Haven't you ever lost yourself in Eric's eyes, in his hair—well, in his scalp, I guess you'd have to say. So young to be so bald."

"One time I lost myself up his left nostril, awful dark in there. Seriously, I'm getting nauseous. Just remember to use condoms, gloves and a large umbrella." I gesture to my textbook. "I'm supposed to be studying the Korean War."

"Really? I thought you were studying hearing loss." Mom gestures to the CD player.

There's a moment of silence as Mom looks at the discs in my CD tower. It's an opening. I could tell her about the phone call, could ask her what to do.

But the words don't come. The moment stretches to the breaking point. And still, nothing. She has told me every secret of her life, every pain and humiliation, every passion and minor joy. She leaves me nowhere to breathe.

And so I can't tell her.

Mom sits on my bed and stretches out her legs. She's worn holes in the heels of her nylons, and one big toe sticks out naked and white. She usually wears killer heels, the higher the better. Nosebleeds, she calls them, because of their elevation. Mom's convinced she's shrinking. I think it's because I'm taller than her now, have been for three years.

"You don't start shrinking until your sixties," I've told her. But she never let facts stick in her way.

On the bus she always stands. She can't take the way her feet don't touch the floor. On an empty bus, she'll stand for twenty blocks.

Mom looks kind of severe. You know, sharp nose and cheekbones. But when she was me, seventeen and free, she must have been pretty hot. With baby fat to soften her face, unwrinkled, unworried.

"Mom," I say. "You must have been one fine piece of jailbait."

She frowns, but takes the compliment. I don't hand them out too often.

Mom picks up a Jimi Hendrix CD and reads the liner notes. "I remember when this came out a million years ago. It's so old."

"You're the one who's old, Mom. Jimi ain't aged a day."

"This fossil has a few moves left. Right now I'm moving downstairs for some popcorn. What do you say?" She obviously feels like talking, and she can't do that without me, the Listener.

I push the Korean War away from me. "I say just a pinch of cayenne pepper and drown 'em in butter."

Mom leaves, using the chocolate-bar wrapper to

mark her place in her true-crime slasher book. My eyes travel the walls, yellow, liquid-sunshine walls, and end up where they must have been heading all along. There's a bald patch of gray by the wall socket, big enough to fit the torso of a curious monkey poking his curious finger into the strange electric three-pronged hole. What's left is an arm and a head with a three-hundred-volt shocked frizz and bugged-out eyes.

What's left are a few electric questions. And the answers are dying not so far away. And if there's nothing really there, if the answers are all lies, then there's still the chance to scream the questions.

There's still that chance.

CHAPTER 13

As I stand in line for the Greyhound bus, behind the man smoking a cigar that smells like a burning dog turd, I wonder for the millionth time why I'm going. Still don't have an answer.

Because he's dying. But so what? People die all the time. Why should this matter? Why can't I just forget him? They've got to invent a home lobotomy kit one of these days.

The bus doors open and we start to board, handing our tickets to the driver before stepping inside. He tears mine in half and I go in, passing the point of no return.

I sit by a window and spread my jacket out on the aisle seat beside me. If I'm lucky, I won't have to spend the whole trip with someone leaning and breathing all over me. Outside, other buses pull up, luggage compartments are emptied, drivers hotfoot it to the nearest toilet, disembarking passengers stretch and shuffle their feet, trying to wake their sleeping butts. The window

I'm looking through is tinted, changing the morning light outside to late afternoon. The bus air smells dead, breathed so many times it's lost all nutritional value.

Earlier this morning, I wiped off three shades of lipstick before I stopped to think. What am I doing, making myself up? Is this like a date? Why do I have to look good, or pretty or anything? Why should I lie?

Why? Why? Why?

There's barely a dozen people on the bus. I fish my pocket watch out of my jacket: 11:02 A.M. What's the holdup? We should be moving already.

The watch is old, not antique old, but secondhand. Mom gave it to me. After my father disappeared, Mom went crazy cleaning out the place. His clothes were walking around on street people's backs faster than you can say Salvation Army. She practically dusted the whole house for his fingerprints, and wherever or whatever they were found on was trashed or scrubbed or doused in holy water. She went nuts, but in a healthy way. She said she was going to get her silver diamond engagement ring melted down into a silver bullet just in case he came back. The ring met with a less dramatic fate. She cashed it in at a pawnshop.

And that's where she saw this pocket watch in a display case, already engraved with the initials A.S., which could stand for a lot of things. Handing it to me, Mom said, "Now it stands for Alice Silvers." She told me that seeing the watch lying there, with the money in her hand from the sale of the evil ring, felt like destiny. She couldn't resist.

All this thinking takes up three minutes. It's 11:05. I imagine running up to the driver and yelling, "We've got to get going, it's a matter of life and death!" Which it is, kind of. I want to be there already. I want to be back already. I just want to get moving.

"Morning, Nancy," I hear the driver say. "You're running a little late."

"I was dressed in time, and everything packed. But Billy got sick on the home bus. Am I too late?"

The driver laughs. "Wouldn't leave without you."

This Nancy comes on board. She looks like she's in her twenties, but it's hard to tell. She has this blank expression on her face. Her voice sounded like a little girl's. She must be retarded.

The driver takes his seat and the door closes. Nancy walks down the aisle, touching the edge of the seats she passes with her hand. I can see her whispering something, and as she goes by me I hear her.

"Six. Seven. Eight."

Counting rows. She stops at eight. Her favorite seat, I guess. She takes the window seat and sets her backpack beside her.

What happens if eight is taken? Does she find another? Does she stand?

The bus pulls away. Finally.

Eric wanted to see me off, but I said what good will that do? I told him it would just depress me. I'd probably break down and not go. Besides, I'll be back by seven at the latest. A few hours. I keep telling myself that.

A couple rows ahead of me a guy has earphones on. I can hear the electric buzz, the rise and fall of voices and guitars. The sound draws the focus of my ears like a mosquito.

Yesterday, I asked Rachel if I could keep the tape

with her singing my "Hate You" song. She was thrilled.

"My first recording, a capella. So you really liked it?" she said.

"You have the most beautiful voice," I told her.

She broke out into a smile that turned into a frown. "So you like it?"

I sighed. Rachel's brown eyes looked so soft. I'm sure those eyes have cried gallons of tears. Her emotions are so close to the surface, it's painful to see. Makes me nervous.

"It's an ugly song," I said. "I just think you're too beautiful for it."

Rachel blushed an amazing shade of red. She stared at the floor and for a second I was terrified she might cry.

"I read it over a few times, just speaking it out loud," Rachel said. "And I thought it was really deep and everything. But I just couldn't believe it, you know. For me, I mean. I couldn't say the words and mean them. I couldn't hate like the song hates."

Like you hate, she didn't have to say.

"I just never learned how," she said. "I know that sounds stupid—"

"No. No," I broke in on her. "I think that's the perfect way to say it."

The guy with the earphones flips his tape over. The buzz stops; the mosquito has landed. We're on the highway now, the city shrinking behind us. Cars pass by, silenced by thick windows and the steady thrum of our own engine.

Glancing to my right, I watch Nancy open her backpack. She removes something and holds it in her hand. I can't quite make it out, something small, orange and fluffy. She holds it up to her mouth and licks it. She moves the fluffball a little and licks it again, then twice more. Nancy whispers into her hand and mashes the fluff against her window.

It's one of those old Garfield suction-cup stuffed animals that people used to stick in their car windows. She whispers to it again, pointing to something passing by. Nancy's making a face as if she's licked a hundred stamps. She goes digging in her pack and finds a box of mini Ritz crackers. To take the taste away. She must do this a lot; she comes prepared.

Seeing her traveling alone like this makes me nervous. She's like a child, so vulnerable. Just the thought of Nancy finding her row-eight seat already taken and standing there lost and confused makes my eyes tear up a bit. I know I'm being crazy, but she's sitting there eating her crackers, talking to Garfield, as if there's nothing to be afraid of. As if she's safe. She's on a bus trip with her silent, stuffed companion. And she's fearless.

I feel cold all of a sudden so I button up my jean jacket. I'm wearing a black sweater, jeans, army boots. Nothing my father's ever seen me in before, nothing he'll remember. My secret wish, a secret I'd share only with my trusted soul mate Curious George, is that he won't even recognize me. I'll walk into his hospital room, he'll look over and . . . nothing. Not a surprised expression, no "Is that really you?" Nothing.

I'm someone he's never met. I'm not the kid who held his hand, who screamed wild laughter colliding on the bumper cars, not the kid who was tickled into exhaustion. I'm just a stranger who accidentally shares a last name with him.

I open my pocket watch. Soon. Getting close now. The mosquito two rows ahead is buzzing again. Nancy leans her head against the window, her lips moving occasionally, speaking words meant for stuffed ears only.

CHAPTER 14

Baby-blue halls stretch off in all directions. St. Paul's hospital is set up like a maze, and I'm one lost little mouse searching for the cheese.

I go up to the desk where a woman is staring at a computer screen, chewing furiously on the end of her pen. She's dressed in pale blue, maybe to camouflage her against the pastel walls and save her from stupid questions.

"Hi, I'm looking for a patient," I say.

She frowns at the sound of my voice; then she covers it. I'm used to this, I even expect it. "Which ward?" she asks around her pen.

"I don't know. Wherever they keep the cancer patients."

The woman stops chewing.

"That would be the oncology unit. You're on the wrong floor. Take the elevator up to five, turn right. Ask at the desk there."

I stand in front of the elevator for a full two minutes before remembering to press the button.

The fifth floor is identical to the first. Same maze, same mouse.

"I'm looking for a patient."

"What's the name, please?"

"Silvers. Frank Silvers." I can't remember the last time I spoke that name. It sounds out of place, out of time.

"Here we are. Silvers." The woman studies her screen. "Are you a family member?"

"He's my father."

"Okay. He's in room 521. Down the hall here, make a left and straight down to the end."

Passing room 518 I see a window at the end of the hallway. It's cool, cloudy autumn outside. All the green leaves are bleeding into red and yellow. Their dying colors. A sudden strong desire takes hold of me, to be out there under the trees ankle-deep in leaves. To be cold and blown by the wind, breathing live air, air that moves. I slow down.

You can do this. It's just like holding your breath underwater.

I remember those old Tarzan movies where he'd wrestle this boa constrictor, crocodile or whatever underwater for about ten minutes without coming up for a breath. I always sat there trying to hold my breath as long as Tarzan. He won, of course, but I got pretty good at it. The trick is not to panic.

Room 521. I push the door open and go in.

It's one of those rooms with a drawn curtain sectioning off the two patients. In the bed closer to the door there's an old man sleeping with tubes up his nose. I step carefully over to the curtain, making sure my boots don't squeak against the shiny floor, telling myself not to panic. I can do this.

I peek around the curtain. There's an Asian man reading a newspaper, propped up in bed. He's attached to a group of silent machines, displaying numbers and wavy lines. He gives me a puzzled look.

"Sorry," I say. "Wrong room."

I back up and open the door. The sign says 521.

Oh God! That's him, the old man. I'm frozen for a full minute until I remember to breathe. Edging over to the foot of his bed, I look at the chart hung there. FRANK JAMES SILVERS.

He's breathing shallowly. The tubes up his nose must be oxygen. I try not to think of those nightmare pictures they show you in school of smokers' lungs, all gray and withered. His hair has thinned, gray where it used to be dark brown like mine. His skin has no color, kind of beige. And thin, he's so thin. The one arm lying above the blankets is all bone, with scrawny muscles thin and tight as guitar strings.

I find myself breathing in rhythm with his shallow gasps. Forcing a deep breath into my lungs, I lift a chair from against the wall and set it closer to the bed. Closer but still out of reach.

My legs are shaking bad. I don't think I could stand now if he came at me.

What am I saying? The man's a corpse. An autopsy waiting to happen.

A sound forces its way up my throat, nothing like laughter. It tastes of bile. I bite down on my lip and kill it. If I stare at the floor I'll be all right. The floor in the room is checkered black and white. Black and white and black and white. The pattern calms me. Perfect order.

In the dim, dusty reaches of my brain I remember playing checkers with him. I must have been really young, because I recall standing at the coffee table so I could look down on the board while he sat on the couch on the other side.

"Let's make this interesting," he said (or something like that). "Why play if you're not going to win anything?"

I gave him a blank look. Checkers was like rocket science to me back then.

He ran to the kitchen and came back with a bag of Oreo cookies. "I'll be black," he said, setting up the Oreos on the board. "And you'll be white." He removed the top from half the cookies so the creamy center faced up, tossing the tops back in the bag.

"Now, if you jump one of my blacks you get to eat it. If I jump a white, I eat it. Got it?"

I must have gotten it, because we started playing and eating, moving our pieces through the debris of crumbs.

Just now I realize that the game was rigged. When he jumped one of my pieces he got to eat the sweet cream, where I had to eat the whole dry cookie.

Frank James Silvers coughs in his sleep, sounding like a handsaw biting into wood. It takes a couple of minutes for the wheezing and crackling to die down. The extra effort to breathe brings a slight flush to his cheeks, but even this tiny hint of life doesn't look real, more like the blush the morticians apply to a corpse.

I'm staring at the door, thinking of making a quick

escape, when it swings open. Startled, I jump to my feet, the chair squealing on the floor.

A woman stands in the doorway. She has blond hair frozen with hairspray into a Medusa tangle that's probably supposed to look windblown. She's short, but wearing pumps to make up the difference. Leather jacket. Short skirt. Did someone order a strip-o-gram?

"You're Alice?" she says.

"Uh. Yes. And you're . . . ?"

"I'm Linda. We talked on the phone. Your father's girlfriend." She lets the door close behind her. Stepping over to the side of his bed, she looks down at him. "He's in pretty rough shape. They're pumping all these drugs into him, so he sleeps most of the time. When he's awake, he's kind of delirious, you know. Spacy." Linda gives me a weak smile.

She notices me noticing the way she's dressed.

"I'm dropping by before work," she tells me. "I'm a waitress over at the Rib Club. This is sort of the required uniform. Gets big tips." She reaches over and smooths out a fold in the blankets covering him. "Has he woke up? Said anything?"

"No. Nothing," I say, my voice shaking and cracking.

She takes a couple steps toward me. "You all right, honey?"

My hands go up instinctively to ward her off. "I always sound like this. My voice. It doesn't mean anything."

My father moans. Linda turns to him. His eyes are open, but they look glassy and unfocused. He moans something again, sounds like a word.

She bends down over him, her face close to his.

"Lindy," he manages in a quiet whimper.

"I'm here, honey. Right here." Her eyes well up and a tear falls on his cheek, making him blink. She wipes it away. "Sorry. I'm getting you all messed up."

I can see now that even the color of his eyes has changed, more gray now than blue.

"Someone else is here to see you," Linda tells him. "She's right here." She motions for me to come closer, and I force my legs to obey. "It's Alice. Your daughter, Alice."

Those gray eyes blink and squint, straining in an effort to focus. I stand beside him, beside the hand lying above the covers, and stare down into his eyes, trying to find the memory of my father.

He grunts out a word. "Alley?"

"That's right," Linda says. "Alice is here."

"Alley," another grunt. "Alley Cat."

A short, sharp pain stabs at me inside, as if a splinter I'd swallowed was digging its way out. If I was alone, I'd curl up and stay very still until the feeling disappeared.

Nobody ever called me Alley Cat except him. I've never even thought about that name since he left. This really is him. This gray, dying old man is my father. I watch his eyes fog over and close as he falls back into sleep.

After a minute listening to his weak breathing, Linda pats his hand gently as if it might crumble under that slight pressure. His hands are still big, but the fingers are long and spidery, the tips still stained an ugly yellow.

"I think he's going to sleep awhile now," she says. "Do you want to grab some coffee? I still have time."

I don't drink coffee, but I'll take any excuse to leave this stale little room.

The hospital cafeteria is on the ground floor with a patio. I tell Linda I need fresh air, so we sit outside. She zips up her leather jacket and blows on her coffee. I sit with a tea steaming in my hands, pushing around the leaves under the table with my boots.

"How did you know it was me when you came into the room upstairs?" I ask her.

"Oh. Well . . ." She sets her cup down and picks her bag off the ground. "I keep some of your father's things with me in case he needs them. And . . . here it is."

Linda hands me a wallet-sized photo. It's one of those school pictures with the kid all dressed up and smiling on command. The kid is a girl with long brown hair, hazel eyes, wearing a moss-green sweater.

"It's an old picture, but you still look basically the same. Not as chubby, though." She laughs nervously.

"Where did you find this?" The girl in the photo is impossibly young, the expression on her face is so—I don't know—happy, maybe. Even the smile doesn't look faked.

Linda sips her coffee. "In his wallet. Frank used to show it to me sometimes."

The longer I stare at the picture, the more angry I get. If he kept a photo of me, it should have been the Polaroid of the bruises on my neck, not all this bright-eyes-and-smiles crap. Who's he trying to fool? I drop the photo on the table.

My tea's still way too hot, but I take a quick sip anyway. The burn of it going down feels good, it gives an edge to my anger.

"So how long has he got left?" I say.

She was about to take a drink but sets her cup down. There's lipstick on the rim, some tacky purple-red shade. Must get big tips for her.

"Not long," she says, looking at her coffee.

"Months? Weeks?" I press on. I know I'm being a real witch, but I don't care.

Linda meets my eyes and mutters. "Days, maybe. The doctors say. He's already signed the papers. You know, so he won't be artificially respirated or anything."

Days? Hours? But he hasn't even heard me, heard the freak he strangled me into being. All he knows is this stupid school picture. Sorry, Dad, but that's not who you left behind. That's who you murdered.

Linda takes a long swallow and looks at her watch.

"Look, I know he's not the greatest person or anything," she says. "I know he didn't always treat you right."

"He told you that?"

"He told me enough. But all I mean to say is, he's changed some. Maybe it's only his being sick, but I've gotten to know him over the last couple of years and I don't know that he ever had a choice to be anything but bad. His father was a total monster to him, his mother was this sad drunk." Linda shakes her head and frowns. "What choice did he have?"

I don't want to hear this. This is garbage. Those were his hands on me, nobody else's. Don't tell me he's the victim in all this. You can feel sorry for the corpse upstairs. Waste your own time.

I think all this but hold back from shouting it across the table at her. I have to get out of here, though. Fast.

"I have to catch my bus," I snap, standing up.

"Okay. I guess I should be getting to work too. It was good meeting you."

"Yeah. Bye." I turn and walk quickly across the grass to the street.

I don't know why, but I'm crying. I'm such an idiot. Swiping at the tears, I wait until I'm a few blocks away from the hospital to open my right fist. I flatten out the crumpled school photo of myself and take a last look at it. Then I tear it into the smallest confetti I can and toss it behind me.

CHAPTER 15

"What's this?"

Rachel's being nosy, but I don't mind. Except for Eric I never have anybody over to my place, so there's a definite weirdness to this moment.

She's pointing to a stack of pages bound with three steel rings. I pick it up and heft it with both hands.

"God," she says. "It's big as a phone book."

"It's about as exciting as a phone book too."

I toss it so she has to catch it and feel the weight of the thing.

"Did someone actually write this? This is like a book?" She reads the title on the plain yellow cover. "*Life Between Breaths: Agoraphobia and Art in the Life of Jan Van Woerner.* Gross, I feel like I'm going to learn something just holding this in my hands."

Rachel sits on the couch and lays the book down on the coffee table. "So who's Desiree Reubens?" she says, reading the name off the cover.

"That's my mother's maiden name. I know, she

sounds like she escaped from one of those Tennessee Williams plays."

I remember when I told Mom that, how she busted a gut laughing. How she said she was going to call the story of her life, "My Name Is Desire."

"Your mom wrote this?" Rachel pokes it like she expects it to spring up and attack her. "Why?"

"It's from when she went to university. This monster was her master's thesis, the paper she had to write to get her degree. You know, her M.A.?"

Rachel's all in black, of course. In hiding. The reason I asked her over was because of what Eric said about me maybe being good for her. He didn't buy that I was staying away so I wouldn't hurt her.

"Besides you," Eric told me. "She's the only person I ever sort of felt like I could kind of, you know, love." Then he got all paranoid that he was showing some illegal emotion. "What? Why are you looking at me like I'm nuts?"

I shook my head, smiling at the confusion in his big brown eyes. "I'm not looking at you like you're nuts. You're looking at me like you're nuts." Which I think was a brilliant thing to say. But what response did I get?

"Words!" Eric shrugged in disgust. "Too many words."

So I'm here with Rachel because he loves her and I love him. And maybe because I might like her too, but don't quote me on that.

"So what's 'angoraphobia' mean?" Rachel says, reading the word off the cover of the yellow monster.

"That's when you have this fear of the outside,

so you never ever leave your house. It's actually 'a-goraphobia,' not 'angora-phobia.' 'Angora-phobia' would be like the fear of fluffy sweaters."

She laughs, covering her mouth. She even laughs in the right key. How can I not hate her?

"So, this Jan Van Worms guy couldn't leave the house?" she asks.

"Yeah. Mr. Worms stayed in his room for something like twenty years. He was a painter who just did still lifes. You know, when they paint fruit and vases and just dead stuff. And everything in the picture is supposed to be symbolic. Like sometimes they'll have a pomegranate beside a skull beside a wooden flute. And the skull means death, the flute is the arts and the pomegranate is—I don't know—the fate of the unborn or something."

Rachel makes a face. "I hate symbolism. Gives me a headache. We're doing Hemingway now, and I'm supposed to find all these symbols. But where are they? Why do they hide them in the first place?"

I smile. "I know. I read that one by him where this old guy goes fishing. I finished it and thought: So what? Some geezer catches a fish and loses it. Big deal! Then the teacher says how it's all symbolic. The old guy is supposed to be Christ and the sharks are the evils of the world or something. Where does it say that? Did my copy have some pages stuck together, or what? Why don't they just tell you straight out instead of hiding everything?"

We shake our heads together, then everything gets real quiet. Too quiet. Rachel starts chewing her lower lip.

"So your mom does art?" she says.

"Mostly backgrounds for plays. And some dioramas for the City Museum. Stuff like that."

I can tell Rachel's going to cardiac arrest if it gets too quiet.

"You want to see something she did? A painting?" Mom would be thrilled to hear me talking about her.

I take Rachel up to my room. It's a wreck, a crash site for a laundry plane. Clearing a path through the toxic waste and general debris, I rummage in my desk drawer. Rachel's standing in the doorway, not entering. At first I think she's horrified by the sight or the stench. But then I see her eyes are tearing up.

Oh God! Don't cry. What did I do wrong? I'm sorry. Whatever it is, I'm sorry. Just don't cry. I'm not good at this.

"What's wrong?" I say.

She sniffles and stares at her feet. "Nothing. I'm just being stupid."

I go back to looking in the drawer so I'm not staring at her. "Did I say something? Is it the smell?"

She laughs a wet laugh. I can hear her runny nose. "Could be the smell," she says.

While I search, Rachel sponges off her face. The storm has passed, I hope. Whatever it was about, I don't need to know.

"Here it is," I say. "Grab a seat on anything that doesn't move."

She sits on the edge of the foot of my bed. Her right hand holds on to her ponytail like a security blanket. What has her so freaked? I set the shoe box I was searching for down between us and rest my hands on top.

"There's a revoltingly cute story that goes with this," I tell her. "I was, I don't know, five or six. I think it was spring. Anyway, I go to my mother and ask for a pear. She says they're out of season, you have to wait until late summer, fall. So I go nuts and start bawling. A season is eternity. And I'll die without this pear. So to shut me up, she says she'll try and make one for me from scratch."

I lift the lid off the shoe box a crack so Rachel can't see inside. Shuffling through the contents of the box, I pull out my flat, two-dimensional pear.

It's painted on a palm-sized piece of paperboard. A pear, perfectly unbruised, the stem attached at the top curved like a question mark.

I give it to Rachel. She holds it with her fingertips like it's an antique, tilting it this way and that, searching for a third dimension.

"This is like a still life?" she says.

"Almost."

"Why almost?"

"Look on the stem."

This is the same game Mom played with me that first time she showed me the pear.

"Why? What's . . . ?" Rachel squints at the pear the size of a playing card. "There's . . . what's that? A little buggy thing."

Crawling on the stem is a tiny orange fire ant. Hidden in plain sight. It could squeeze through the eye of a fat needle. I tell Rachel how Mom painted it with this detail brush that has like three hairs on it. If you look really close, you can see two pinprick dots of white where the ant's eyes catch the light.

"So then I asked for a peach, a raspberry, a kiwi." I

show her the other 2-D fruits, all with an insect hidden but not hidden, there if you look close. After the first couple, Mom made it so only part of the bug was showing, or camouflaged like the ladybug peeking around the side of a raspberry. Mom says the guy who does *Where's Waldo?* stole her idea.

"What's your mother like?" Rachel asks.

"I don't know. She's okay."

Mom's ears must be spontaneously combusting with all this talking about her. I put the stuff away, close the box and tap my fingers on the lid.

"So," I say. "That's it." Show-and-tell's over.

There's a silence that stretches a few beats too long.

Don't ask the question, I tell myself. Just stop. You don't need to know.

"What, um . . . I mean, why were you choking up when you came in the room? It can't be just the smell."

Rachel's grip tightens on her ponytail.

"I was being stupid. It's just that seeing your room—I don't know—it's like I feel I could live here. For years, you know. I could stay in one place for a while. In my last school we read that Hemingway book, *A Moveable Feast.* That's me, a moveable feast. Moving and eating is all I ever do."

Oh God! She's crying. Why am I so stupid? Eric's not the only one who's bad at serious moments.

I put my hand on her shoulder, slowly, like I might get burned. She leans into me, shaking only a little. I'm not good at this. But I reach up and touch her orange hair. I brush it lightly like I'm petting a scared cat. A big scared orange tabby. Her weight presses against me and I can feel the hollow she makes on my bed. For now at least, she is unmoveable.

CHAPTER 16

The deep rumble of an approaching train vibrates my chair. There's a constant rhythm to the clacking and gasping of the steam engine. It feels like I'm going to be run over any time now.

"Tone down the train noise," shouts the director to the sound booth backstage.

The locomotive recedes into the distance.

"A little more. Stop. That's good."

I'm sitting halfway back in the empty audience. A handful of people sit in the first few rows, taking notes, making adjustments. There's Mom off to the side with the art director. This is an early run-through, working out the kinks in the production. It's Saturday afternoon and they're still going strong, so I guess they must be behind schedule. I don't see that Andrew Warner anywhere.

I'm supposed to be having lunch with Mom when they break. She's been seeing this Warner guy a lot, but I've been too busy worrying about everything happening in my own wretched life to notice much. There's a twenty-year difference between them. When she was thirty, he was only ten. It's too weird.

The director is making big sweeping gestures with his arms, indicating changes he wants in the set. Everyone nods, tells him how brilliant he is and takes notes.

The whole setup for *Last Train Leaving* looks pretty neat. Center stage is the passenger compartment where the whole play will take place. There's a polished wooden bench facing the audience. Empty now, they won't start rehearsals on the set for another week.

"Can we try the projection?" the director shouts past me toward the back of the theater. A couple of stagehands pull the long, straight white drapes together to where they converge on either side of the compartment. The lights dim and the clicking light of the projector reveals a distant shot of a steam train traveling through an afternoon landscape. Someone makes adjustments and the image stretches and widens to cover the entire stage. The effect is dreamlike. If you were sitting on the bench staring outward, you would be blinded by the wavering light, but if you glanced around yourself you'd see trees and mountains and tracks printed on your clothes and skin; you would be the screen.

A cell phone starts ringing. Someone talks way too loud, deafening the caller.

"Lights! Can we bring up the lights?" It's the director shouting. He's the one screaming into the phone.

The lights come up.

He tosses the phone to one of his underlings. "Lunch, everybody. One hour."

I walk down the aisle, wading through the outgoing tide of theater people. Mom is gathering her portfolio together, juggling two clipboards, a sketchpad and a handful of pencils, pens and markers.

"What a lazy bum," I say. "And here I thought you worked for a living."

"Grab something. Anything. Before I fall apart."

I take her clipboards while she wrestles everything else into her case. "I'm starving," she tells me. "Do you think this will be safe if I leave it here? No, I better take it with me or I'll worry all through lunch."

She peeks in on Warner in the projection booth, but he's too busy splicing film to take a lunch break.

"Aren't you supposed to be giving him guidance or something?" I say. "So he gets his extra credit or whatever?"

"He knows what he's doing. It looked great, didn't it? Even the director liked it. I know, it's hard to tell, but that's the way he looks when he's pleased."

Outside, the wind's whipping up a first taste of winter. Mom's huge portfolio acts like a sail as she's blown ahead of me down the sidewalk. Mom looks like slapstick waiting to happen.

"Where are we going?" I yell ahead.

"Wherever the wind takes us," she shouts back.

We end up in a dingy little diner that's never heard of health codes. Mom manages to wedge her case between the stools and the counter and we look at a menu that's been spilled on, fingerprinted with grease and other ungodly things.

"How about the *soup du jour*?" I point to a chalk-smeared blackboard.

"I don't want to get intestinal parasites." She flips the menu over, then tosses it to the side. "Oh, look. They have chocolate bars and potato chips."

I'm halfway through a big bag of Chee-tos and Mom's on her third Kit Kat, washing it down with coffee. Lunch of Champions.

"You know," she says. "David Berkowitz—the Son of Sam killer—tried to use a sugar high to explain his murderous rampages."

Who the hell actually says "murderous rampages"? Mom talks like she's anchoring the nightly news sometimes.

"That was his legal defense," she goes on. "I think it was called the Twinkie Defense. I can see how you might get a little shaky, but that's no reason to start shooting strangers."

I sigh. Lunch with Mother.

"Of course, he also claimed a neighbor's dog was the devil and told him to do those evil things." She finishes by stuffing two Kit Kat fingers in her mouth.

"Lovely," I say. "I'm glad we can spend this quality time together."

"Don't be like that. So, why the big visit?" she asks me finally. "Something wrong?"

I want to get some answers from her—I just don't know how to ask the questions. I wipe my orange-tipped fingers on a napkin. They stay a little yellow, like smoker's fingers.

"Can't I come see my dearest mother without a reason?"

She gives me a doubtful look.

I lick my fingers and wipe them again.

Forget it. Just tell her.

"Someone phoned one night about a week ago, when you were at the theater. It was a woman. She, um, was calling to tell me that Frank Silvers is in the hospital."

A Dead Zone settles in the space between us. She sets her chocolate bar on the counter. The quiet stretches until I'm ready to break. Then she closes her eyes. "Frank?"

"My father," I add stupidly. There are millions of Franks but only one who means anything.

"He's sick?" Her eyes are lifeless, cold. An enormous distance has come between us with the mention of that name.

"He's dying," I say.

So I tell her the whole thing—the call, the bus trip, the corpse, his girlfriend.

Mom sits completely still, as if she's surrounded by sharp edges and any move will cause her pain. I'm talking more than I should, running on, afraid to stop and be faced by her silence.

"He kept that picture of me. That stupid old school thing. I must have been in the fifth grade or something. And he kept it." I stop and meet her eyes for a second. Nothing. She's not speaking. So I ask her: "Why? Why would he keep that?"

Mom won't ignore a direct question from me. She doesn't even need a second to think about it.

"Because," she says. "That's how he wants to keep you. His pretty little smiling girl. He doesn't want to remember what he did to you. Me, he's probably worked it out in his head that I was asking for it. I made him do it. But you were perfect, innocent. He doesn't want to believe what he did to you."

Mom gets a refill on her coffee, drinks it too fast and burns her lip. "Stupid," she mutters to herself.

"You wouldn't even recognize him anymore. He's this shriveled old man."

Mom licks her hurting lip. "I'd recognize him if he was just a skeleton. I can't forget. What he did to you, that was my fault."

I shake my head, but she waves it away with her hand.

"Don't say anything. It's true. I should have gotten us out of there a long time before that. I was just too stupid, that's all. From the start."

I hate seeing Mom torturing herself. But there's nothing I can say to stop it, nothing she will believe.

"You'd think I'd get used to your voice after all these years." Mom's eyes look dangerously wet. God, don't cry. Please don't. "But I can't. I know the way you used to sound, your real voice. It kills me."

The first tear falls down her cheek. I scrabble at the napkin dispenser and shove a handful at her.

"Not here, Mom," I say, amazed at how cruel I sound. "Drink your coffee."

She obeys like a little kid, taking a long sip. I suddenly feel so angry. It kills *her*? My voice? Well, good. It should kill her. It kills me every day. I try to tell myself that Mom's not the one I hate, but I really don't know anymore. Maybe I hate her and him and everybody. Maybe that's all I have inside.

I look outside at the people on the street being blasted by frigid winter air. They lean into the wind, either fighting it to move forward, or letting it shove them wherever it wants. I want to get out of here and take my chances with the wind.

Mom's got ahold of herself again. "Sorry," she says, wiping her nose.

"You should be getting back. Don't want to be late," I tell her.

She sniffles. I look the other way. "I'm going to pop into the washroom and get cleaned up. Be right back."

When she's gone, I realize I've been digging my fingernails into my palms. Relaxing my hands, I see where they almost broke the skin. I'm not going to cry with her over how warped and freakish I am. That's a solo act.

We walk back. The wind is a good excuse for silence. Mom looks so small, gusting along with her huge portfolio like a child with an adult's briefcase. And for one instant I want to reach out and steady her, protect her. But protecting is supposed to be her job. Was supposed to be her job. Not mine.

CHAPTER 17

Eric has an acoustic guitar he drags out of the closet now and then to torture me with. He knows exactly how awful he sounds; he just doesn't care.

"Just making some noise, that's all that matters," he sings above the stumbling chords. Eric has no shame. I think he figures that I've seen him at his stupidest and that didn't kill my affections, so nothing will.

"How about I make some noise by beating that thing upside your head?" I say.

He finishes on one fading discordant note.

"The audience goes wild. Women's underwear rains down on the stage."

I groan. "Is this really what's going on in that cue-ball head of yours?"

"Don't get jealous. I'll give the underwear back."

We have about an hour alone before his parents get home from work. This is how he wants to waste it.

I went through today at school in a trance, in a blur of tangents and cosines and Nixon's Vietnam policy, until I got to my locker after last class, dragging the atomic weight of my tired brain, and couldn't recall my combination. Luckily, Eric came along and did it for me.

I didn't sleep last night. My father was waiting for me behind my closed eyelids, all scrawny, gray and gasping.

"So, are you going to talk?" Eric asks, tossing the guitar on his bed.

"What about?"

"Come on, how did it go?"

"It went." I shrug. "I don't know."

"What was he like?"

I rub my face, trying to wipe away the sleepy fog clouding my brain.

"He was always a jerk. Now he's a dying jerk."

Eric scratches his stubbly head. "So you talked to him?"

"Not really. He was kind of beyond talking when I saw him. He grunted a few words. Nothing I want to talk about. It won't help anything."

He stands up. "Okay. I tried to melt the ice queen. Can't say I didn't try." Eric goes over and grabs a CD from the top of a pile by his player. "A present for Her Frigid Highness."

He picks up a CD and hands it over to me. *Small Change,* it's called, by someone named Tom Waits.

"Never heard of him," I say.

"I know, I just discovered him the other day. I was in a used-CD place and they were playing this." Eric takes it from me and slides it into the player, cranking the volume. He gives me the liner notes to look at.

It doesn't look promising. The cover photo shows a scraggly bearded guy in a haze of cigarette smoke sitting in the dressing room of what looks like a strip bar. (There's a stripper in a G-string in the background, looking bored.)

Quiet piano music starts up. I glance at the notes again, wondering if Eric's got the discs mixed up. But then the singing starts.

The first thing that hits me is the ugliness of this man's voice—a scratched, pitted, croaking voice. He sounds like a drunk, his alcohol-burned vocal chords aged centuries by thousands of unfiltered cigarettes. He sounds like he'll black out before the end of the song, like he's been dragged behind a car in a drunken haze. The lyrics are about losers and late-night fights at run-down joints.

The longer I listen, the more I realize that Tom Waits knows exactly what he's doing. The songs are hopeless and funny and smart. And only with that horrible voice would they ever sound believable. It's like he's ugly by nature, but also ugly on purpose, to make his point.

Then it strikes me. I drop the notes on the floor. These songs, they wouldn't mean anything unless he sang them that way. They have to be ugly. He has to sound ripped and burned. Anything less would be a lie.

I grab my jacket off the bed.

"Bring your guitar, baldy. We're going over to my place."

I've never heard myself at full volume before, so my first reaction is to break down and die right there. The speakers magnify my imperfections, leaving me nowhere to hide. Every crack and wild note is caught and focused. It takes a supreme effort to hear the song I'm singing without hating myself at the same time.

On the third playback, I start to hear it without my own feelings getting in the way. It's a crappy recording we just did on tape using my stereo, me singing and Eric playing bad guitar. My song "Hate You." It sounds ugly and painful, my voice totally out of control.

And it's perfect.

I never saw it before, couldn't get past myself. But this is how it has to be to make it real. It's not going to work with a normal voice.

"Do you hear it?" I ask Eric, who's lying on my bed staring at the yellow ceiling.

"I hear it."

"What do you think?"

He grabs me and pulls me down on the bed beside him. "I think it sounds like the truth. It bleeds, you know, it really bleeds."

I have a voice! An ugly, ragged, dragged-through-the-dirt voice. But it's real. It's mine.

I jump up to rewind the tape and hear it again, but stop myself.

"Let's try another song. What do you say?"

"The audience goes wild," he says. "The audience goes wild."

CHAPTER 18

Because he's never heard my voice. That's why I find myself on that bus again, on the long warped winding road to St. Paul's hospital.

"He doesn't want to believe," Mom said to me. If I have to steal his last breath, I'll make him remember. I live with those memories, and if he's not able to live with them too, then at least he can die with them.

Listen to me—what a psycho!

Leaning my head on the cold window, I watch the bald gray highway pass by. There are houses set alongside it, blocked by two-story-high barriers to kill the noise. Still there must be a constant rumble that penetrates inside the houses. You would get used to it, I guess, until you forgot it completely the way you forget about breathing and blinking. The way you forget the sound of your own voice until you hear it coming back at you.

I wish that woman was here, riding along with me eating Ritz crackers and chatting up her stuffed companion. Nancy, that was her name. I'm sitting in the same seat as last time, but she's missing. Row eight is empty. Wherever she is, I'm sure Garfield with his suction hands is close by.

Last time I was on this bus I hoped Frank Silvers wouldn't even recognize me, that I'd look like a stranger to him. "Alley Cat," he called me, staring with those gray, doped-up eyes. Hearing that name cracked some tiny, insignificant bone inside me. Something close to my heart. That's how it felt.

Now, I want him to see me. Not some shadow of a ten-year-old, no smiling little girl. See me! Even if I have to scream it through his sleep-drugged haze.

I can imagine half a dozen nurses dragging me kicking and spitting off to the psycho ward. What did Eric say? "Off to the rubber room and the shirts that tie in the back." I can't help a small grin, thinking of Eric's stupid little smile. His crew cut is getting out of control. I should shave him clean again. Taking care of someone like that, doing something so basic for him, makes me feel impossibly close to Eric, so needed. It's one of the things that holds me together.

I shake off the warm feeling that threatens to overtake me when I think of Eric. I have to be numb and rigid now or I'll never go through with it.

What if Frank Silvers is already dead? He was hanging on by the thinnest of threads as it was. "Days," was what that Linda woman said he had left. What if he's dead? No. That's not an option. He can't die until he really hears me.

St. Paul's is an old place. A brass plaque says it was built in 1908. I'd be nervous getting delicate surgery in such an ancient building, like getting a boob job at the

Acropolis. There are signs everywhere telling you you're in a HOSPITAL QUIET ZONE. And here's me without my slippers, stomping along in army boots. Cars still drive by, roaring, honking and belching. The world speeds on. "Quiet Zone" is wishful thinking.

After all this rush, I'm killing time circling the block.

Just rip it right off! I tell myself. Don't tug at it so you feel every hair and skin cell being torn away. Do it fast. One quick motion. Don't look back.

The doors slide themselves open as I approach. There are decals on the bottom of the glass panels. INVISIBLE DOORMAN, they say. As if there's a ghost who lives to open and close these doors, a former patient working off his medical bills into the afterlife. Maybe I should leave an invisible tip.

I walk down the calm blue halls. It must be a slow day, no major disasters or murderous rampages. Mom would be so disappointed. As I take the elevator up to five, the air seems to get thinner, as if I'm climbing straight to the top of a mountain. I'm breathing hard when I get out. Tarzan would be ashamed of me. Here he spends ten minutes battling giant lizards and rib-crushing snakes underwater and I wimp out inhaling sterilized air on the elevator. Not funny. Nothing's funny here.

Don't let him see you like this, I tell myself.

I find room 521. I take a deep breath, hold it and push the door open.

He's still there. The skin of his face seems to sink into every hollow and cavity of his features, losing its form to the gravity pulling him deeper down into his pillow. His skin hangs like pajamas on a scarecrow.

He's hooked up to more machines than last time. No artificial respirator, though. There's an IV in his arm, tubes up his nose, half a dozen electrode-tipped tentacles stuck to him, maybe even a catheter (I don't want to know).

He's awake, barely. His eyelids are heavy, threatening to shut any second. When I step into the room, they turn toward me in slow motion. His neck twists with a tremendous effort.

Those gray eyes stare at me without recognition. His brain exists in a foggy, pain-killed dimension.

"It's me. Alice." I speak slowly and loudly so he'll understand, but also so he'll hear my voice.

He grunts and shakes his head no.

No what? No, I'm not Alice? No, you don't understand?

He blinks a few times as if he's trying to clear his vision and squints at me. My father always had wrinkles, from smoking and everything, but now they've taken over his face. His skin looks like it's about to crack into pieces along a hundred razored lines.

"It's Alice," I repeat.

He manages to whisper something I can't catch. I move closer a tiny bit. Baby steps.

"What was that?"

Again the wheezing whisper. I force myself to go up to the side of his bed. His arms are folded just below the chest, all ready and set for the coffin. Carefully making sure no part of me touches him, not even my hair, I bend to hear him. My heart is seizing up on me. I'm sweating and holding back a shiver at the same time.

"Alley Cat." I can just make out his words now.

Why does he have to keep calling me that? I haven't been Alley Cat since I was ten; that's almost half my life ago. The name confuses me. I used to love him calling me that; it was like a secret password between us.

Doesn't he remember what he did? How can he still call me that? I'm so close to him now—way too close—that I can smell the death in him. It's sweating and breathing out of him. I feel shaky.

"Be an angel," he croaks. "My water." He moves his eyes toward the bedside table, where a plastic cup sits with a straw sticking out.

You want me to feed you—or water you or whatever? I want to scream, but he looks so pathetic. I check the cup. It's half full. My hands are shaking, and it takes everything in me to pick up the cup without spilling it all. It scares me to see myself right on the edge of losing control. It's like watching an explosion in slow motion.

"You want your water?" I have to keep talking, even though my voice is wilder than ever.

"Yeah." His chapped lips open, waiting.

I stick the straw in his mouth and he takes sips between breaths. I'm holding my breath again. I have to stop that; it's making me dizzy, making me shake more. My vision goes blurry as my eyes well up. I can't stop it. Two tears fall before I can wipe them away. One falls on the sheets, the other hits the sleeve of his pajamas where his right biceps would be if he had any muscle left.

He stops drinking, then mumbles into the straw. I put the cup back on the table.

"What's that?" I say, sniffling and covering my face with my hand.

He makes an effort to mumble louder. "Don't do that. That's all Linda ever does." He pauses to get another breath. "Anymore."

A white-hot spark flares up inside me. Don't do that, you tell me? How many times did I tell you don't do that? How many times did Mom?

"Sorry to bother you with my stupid crying! Sorry to take up your time!" My voice has gone insane, hitting trembling high notes. "And I'm sorry I sound like this. But this is what you did to me! You and your hands!"

I wish I could scream at the man he was years ago, when it all happened, back when he was healthy and I was Alley Cat. But this is all that's left.

"How could you *do that to me*? How could . . . ? How?" My throat shuts down and I can't force any more words out.

He's shrunk deeper into his pillow, trying to escape. His breath comes in gasps.

The man on the other side of the curtains must be pressing some emergency nurse alarm, because one rushes in then. She sees me crying and puts her hand on my arm.

"Miss, are you all right?" She looks back and forth between me and my father. "Why don't you come with me? You can get some coffee and have a seat in the cafeteria."

I shake her hand off. I can't have anyone touching me right now. I nod at her, digging an old Kleenex out of my jacket pocket. The nurse holds the door open.

As I walk out, I take a last look back at him. His eyes are wide now, staring at me. I'm surprised to see fear there. He's scared. Scared of what I said. Maybe even scared of what he knows he did to me. He knows it's the truth.

The nurse watches me get on the elevator like I'm some lunatic, some angel of death come to haunt the barely alive. But I don't care. I escape the maze of halls and run outside into the cold autumn air.

I can breathe again. I don't have to hold it anymore. He heard me. I heard me. Half the ward heard me. But *he* heard me!

CHAPTER 19

I'm on an adrenaline rush all the way home. It's like I've had this decade-long headache that's finally lifted, so I can see clearly now. It's night by the time I get back. Nobody's home. Mom's been working late the last week. We haven't been speaking much since that incident in the diner. Nothing more than "Pass the Cool Whip," or "Where's the brown sugar?"

I feel bad about the whole thing. Maybe I'm expecting her to be more than she can be. I don't know. I want to tell her what happened today, want her to know that he heard me.

I sit in the kitchen waiting for her. I eat half a bag of Oreos, tossing away the tops.

It's almost ten. Mom can't still be working. She must be off somewhere with what's-his-face, Warner. And just the other day she was giving me that "Sex is dead" speech. I guess now it's back from the grave. Night of the Loving Dead.

Upstairs, I hop in the tub for a marathon bath. It's best with an empty house and nobody pounding on the bathroom door demanding entry. A real bath takes time, two hours minimum.

At school in the biology lab they have these anatomical models—basically Barbie and Ken with their skin peeled off. They're used to show where the organs are, circulatory systems and muscular structure. There are thousands of muscles in the human body. By the end of my bath every one of those should be a limp wet noodle, so I step out weak as a newborn pony standing for the first time.

With the CD player on top of the toilet, I play some John Lennon just loud enough to cover the belching and uncontrolled flatulence of traffic noise leaking in from the outside world. "Whatever gets you through the night," John sings. I sing it in my head with him, except I change the words to "Whatever keeps you warm at night." I don't think he'd mind. My voice changes in my head, so sometimes I sound like Sheryl Crow or Cher, sometimes like Julie Andrews or Judy Garland. Those last two were kids when they were "discovered." They had big voices, perfect pitch. I can't watch those old silly musicals anymore. I always cry in the wrong spots. While they're happily running through mountaintop fields over the rainbow, I'm sobbing. Their voices hurt too much.

With my big toe I nudge the tap, adding a little hot to the water. Steam is making the walls sweat.

Whatever keeps you warm at night. Eric is a natural radiator, gives off heat like you wouldn't believe. In the dead of winter when my fingers turn three shades of blue he always takes them under his shirt and lays my palms flat on his stomach. He breathes a little gasp at my touch, but presses my hands in deeper. And I bury my face against his neck, feeling his pulse beating on the bridge of my nose.

The first time he did that our first winter together, he took me by surprise. I tried to pull my ten little icicles away but he held them steady.

"It's all right," he told me.

"You'll catch pneumonia."

"Then I'll burn up in the fever of our love."

I stuck one freezing fingertip in his belly button and he let out a little squeak.

The first time he did that with my hands I asked him, "What do you think of my voice?" I'd been thinking of asking him for months, but now I just had to know.

He frowned and took way too long answering.

"It's your voice," he finally said, with a small shrug. "It's you."

"What does that mean?"

"I mean, it's the only you there is. I love your voice. Because it's yours. God, that sounds stupid. I'm not really good at this stuff, saying things."

My hands were heating up. I flexed the waking fingers.

"But it's broken," I said. "My voice is warped. Eric. Eric. See, I can't even say your name without it freaking out on me."

He smiled. "Only you say my name like that. Only you. What else matters?"

That was the first time I ever got a real answer to that question out of anybody. The usual answer was: "You don't sound so bad." But Eric didn't say my voice was good, bad or anything. Just that it was me. What else matters?

I rise from my bath, bright pink and wrinkled, pull the plug and drag my weary bones to bed. I stare at the ceiling. Even in the dark I can still feel my yellow walls.

Over by the wall socket, even in the dark, I can make out the bald patch where the paint's been scraped down to gray. Curious George (my primate soul mate) is there, battered and half chipped away. He'll always be reaching his curious finger into curious places. Nothing can stop him. Or me.

CHAPTER 20

At lunch me and Eric head over to the 7-Eleven. I'm badly in need of a sugar rush. He heads to the back for one of his Jumbo Slushie abominations, where he measures it out so he gets a third Cherry Coke, a third root beer and a third Orange Crush. He has no class.

I grab a couple of candy bars and wait for the carbonated chemist to finish his formula. I'm about to hurry him up when I get this really weird feeling—sort of like déjà vu, where you feel like what's happening has happened exactly the same way already.

Except this is more like a shiver deep in my brain, and I just know positively that something somewhere has gone wrong. Something big.

Dad. The thought hits me suddenly. My father. I think. I think he's dead.

I shove the candy bars in Eric's hand.

"I've got to find a phone fast."

Then I'm outside running down the block. There's

a booth on the corner. My hands are shaking so bad, I can barely get the change out of my pocket without scattering it.

"I need the number for St. Paul's hospital," I tell the operator.

"One moment, please."

She gives me the number. I punch it in.

"St. Paul's, registration desk."

"I'm calling about a patient there. I need to know his condition."

"Which ward is he on?"

"Um, what do you call it? The oncology unit? You know, on the fifth floor."

"All right. I'll transfer your call."

It rings. I lean against the glass side of the booth. Eric is right outside watching me, frowning.

"Fifth floor. Main desk."

"You have a patient there. I have to know how he is. I'm his daughter."

"What's the name, please?"

"Frank Silvers."

"Please hold."

I can't hold. Just tell me already. He's right down the hall. Just go and look.

I'm on hold so long I start to think I've been cut off. But then a different voice comes on the line.

"Hello? Alice?" The voice says.

"Yes? Who's this?"

"It's Linda Rossetti. Your dad's girlfriend." Her voice sounds breathless, like she's been crying.

"Oh. My father, what's his condition?"

All I hear is breathing on the other end.

"Hello?" I say.

"Your father . . . he died just a few minutes ago. I'm so sorry."

I hang up.

Outside, Eric is waiting. "What's wrong?"

I step up close to him. He opens his arms and hugs me as best he can with his hands full of chocolate and slush.

Mom didn't come home at all last night. She missed breakfast, too. The silence of the tomb filled the house. The crunching of Frosted Flakes echoed down the deserted halls and empty rooms as I ate, trying not to slurp and disturb the ghosts. It's not like her. Even when she has her month-long tender, torrid romances, she always comes home at night. It's an unwritten rule.

I'm sitting at the kitchen table, flipping through a bunch of Mom's magazines. I don't know what I'm reading or looking at. My mind is blurry and distracted.

I trashed the rest of the day after that lunchtime phone call. Me and Eric walked around downtown for a few hours going nowhere until I figured Mom would be getting home. Eric wanted me to stay with him, go over to his place, but the only person on the planet I wanted to speak to was Mom. I didn't tell him that. He wouldn't understand. I don't know if I understand.

I'm halfway through an article on Brad Cruise or Tom Pitt when I hear the front door opening and closing. I sit there silently. She doesn't call out, but my boots are on the mat by the door so she must know I'm home. Listening, trying to hear where her footsteps are leading, I'm still startled when she appears in the kitchen doorway.

"Hi," she says, looking so awkward standing there, as if this isn't her house, her daughter, her life she's walked in on.

"Hi. You okay?" I say.

"Yeah. Fine."

"Didn't come home last night."

She shrugs. It's crazy how we seem to have switched roles somehow. She's the surly teenager, and I'm the mother waiting at the kitchen table.

"I got tied up at work," she tells me.

"Warner tied you up? Kinky."

Her face breaks into a smile in spite of itself.

I go over to the fridge. "There's some Black Forest cake left. Shall we?"

Mom tosses her coat on the back of a chair. "Don't be stingy with the Cool Whip," she says.

I make up two obscene plates, with enough fat to cardiac arrest a herd of buffalo. I get her talking about the play and everything, so we slowly ease back into our twisted idea of normal, everyday life.

When we're fully gorged and slightly nauseous, I tell her about going back to St. Paul's. I get to the part where he told me to stop crying—when I lost it and started screaming at him. Mom watches me, her eyes tearing up.

"He heard me. In the end I saw his face. He heard. You know, I could tell I really got through to him." My voice goes so wild I can barely get the words out. But I can see Mom's getting what I'm saying.

Is she crying? I can't tell because tears are blurring my own eyes. I feel like I just sprinted half a mile. My brain is still sprinting. A hundred things flash by in my head, things I want to say to her.

I forgive you, I want to tell Mom. For everything. For not stopping him. For not shutting up when he was angry. For never hiding the bruises he left on you. For not saving me. I want to say so much.

"The other day in the restaurant, I was so cruel to you," I tell her. "I know you did your best for me."

Mom goes over to the sink, rips off some paper towels and buries her face in them. She tries to catch her breath. I think what I just said knocked some of the wind out of her. I hold on to the table and try to stop shaking so much.

Mom hands me a paper towel. I use it to kill the flood and blow my nose. She stands beside my chair, resting one hand on my shoulder, wiping her face with the other.

"At lunch I got this weird feeling," I tell her. "Like something bad had happened to someone, you know? And so I ran and called the hospital. And they told me he's dead. Today at lunch, he died. It was like I felt a little bit of his dying. It's stupid, I know."

"Shhh. I think maybe that bad feelings can tie you to someone as much as good ones can. If you feel strongly enough."

I rub my eyes, glad for the roughness of the paper towel against my skin.

"I hate him. For so long I've hated him. Now there's nothing left to hate."

Mom's hand feels hot on my shoulder, as if all my blood is rushing to that point of contact. I reach up and cover her hand with mine. The last time we held hands, hers were so big they swallowed mine. Now our hands are the same size.

NO ONE COMES LOOKING

There's a boy in the attic
Pulling the wings off angels
His brain filled with static
Hiding in the dark
Waiting for the spark
That'll burn his whole world down

No one comes looking here
No one wants to find him
Doesn't matter where he's gone
There's nothing to remind them
And no one comes looking here
No one comes looking

All he knows is
A slap is a touch
A punch is a touch
The hand that breaks
And shakes is a touch
And nothing he can do
Will matter that much
Because

No one comes looking here
No one comes looking
No one comes

All the wingless angels
Surround him asking why
Listen to him cry
In that old gray room
He dreams his name carved
On a small gray tomb

And no one comes looking here
No one comes

CHAPTER 21

"This is how Elvis started out," Eric tells me.

We're standing in a booth inside a neon monster downtown called Karaoke Krush. There's a thick binder full of popular-song lyrics chained to the counter and one of those heat-sensitive computer screens you touch to choose a tune from the song list.

"I don't think Elvis ever sang 'Girls Just Wanna Have Fun,' " I say, paging through the binder. It's like a record of musical atrocities with a ten-page section devoted to the Bee Gees.

Eric leans his guitar case against the closed door. "Elvis went to the recording studios at Sun Records in Memphis to make a record of his mother's favorite songs for her birthday. That's how he was discovered."

I poke the screen, scrolling through the prerecorded music over which you do your vocal voodoo.

"I just want to get through this without getting arrested," I say.

Eric straps on his guitar. We agreed on something simple for his instrumentals, impossible to screw up.

Pushing the binder aside, I read the instructions on the screen. You get two songs recorded on a CD for twenty bucks. You can screw up and go back again, thank God. I unfold the sheet of paper with "No One Comes Looking" on it, pressing it flat on the counter.

"No one. No one comes." I try the words out softly, then louder. "No one comes looking."

My voice is still disobeying my every command. I wrote this song the day after my father died, which was . . . what? A week ago? Just a week? It feels like forever.

Eric read it. Liked it. He didn't really get it, but I didn't fill him in.

It's about something my father's girlfriend told me. She said his father was a total monster to him, and his mother was this sad drunk.

"What choice did he have?" That's what she said to me. What choice did he have?

That part is crap. I don't care who you are or what's killing you inside, there's always a choice.

But the other, "total monster sad drunk" part, that's what I was thinking of when the song came to me. "There's a boy in the attic/ Pulling the wings off angels." And that boy might be Frank Silvers. A little bit anyway. It was a hard one to write and I don't know how it's going to sound. I just know my vocals are the only ones that can make it work.

Eric nudges me with the arm of his guitar. "I think Meat Loaf is next, waiting in the lobby. We gonna make some music?"

CHAPTER 22

It looks like a train ticket, except that beside "Destination" it says: "*Last Train Leaving.* A PlayDead Production." Under "Departure" it says 8 P.M., which is when the play starts; under "Arrival" it says 9:30, when it ends. It was Mom's idea, doing the tickets this way. I make sure the guy at the door doesn't tear the ticket, so I can keep it.

It's opening night. Mom gave me two tickets, thinking I'd bring Eric, like I did with her last play.

"I think I'm going to have a headache that day," Eric said when I told him about the play.

"Opening night's still a week away."

"Just tell her I've got the flu, or ringworm or something. That last play did pain to my brain. I can't take another one."

"What are you complaining about? You got to stare at a naked woman onstage for two hours," I said.

"Yeah, but you wouldn't let me use the opera glasses."

So I brought Rachel, who's so thrilled to be here,

she's getting me excited too. I like that about her—she's emotionally contagious.

"I've never been to a play before, ever," Rachel says. "Do we have good seats?"

I nod. "Dead center. Third row."

She's wearing this purple suit jacket over black T-shirt and jeans. We discovered the jacket at Value Village, a thrift store. I had to beg to get her to even try it on.

"But it's purple," Rachel said. "I wear black."

I held it out for her to slip into.

"It's too bright," she protested.

"You think gray is too bright."

"It's probably too small."

"Only one way to find out," I said.

I twisted her to the breaking point and finally got her into it.

"It's a keeper," I told her.

"You think? But where am I going to wear it?"

We find our seats. Mom's backstage somewhere. She's kind of an Art Director 911, on call in case a prop explodes or the set collapses. On nights like these she keeps a big bag of M&M's in her pocket to stay on a constant sugar high.

Rachel sits up straight, holding the play program in her lap like she's in church.

"So I bought a poster yesterday," she tells me.

"A poster? You're actually going to put something up on your wall?"

Rachel nods.

"Have you gone nuts?"

She keeps nodding.

"I know, I've been getting pretty radical. You're a

bad influence. Purple jackets! Posters! Next I'll be getting my eyelids pierced."

I laugh. "How about a tongue tattoo?"

The lights flicker twice. It's five minutes to curtain.

"So," I say. "A poster of what?"

"It's this painting by some Belgian guy, Magritte, of a room with a giant green apple taking up the whole room. And there's one window you can see a grassy field out of. I don't know why I like it so much. It's kind of surreal. But however the apple got in there, they'll never get it out. It's symbolic. I mean, for me at least."

"You're the green apple?"

A man in the next row glances back, giving us a look like we're insane. I speak lower.

"I'm the giant fruit," Rachel whispers. "What are those green apples called?"

"Granny Smiths?"

"Right. I'm Granny Rachel. Did I tell you about my mother? She brought home this book of wallpaper patterns. She wants to paper the house. They had a big fight, my mom and dad."

"Over wallpaper?"

"Sort of. My mom's tired of moving around all the time. She finally blew up. Wallpaper is her way of saying we're staying."

The lights start to slowly dim and the voices in the audience die down.

"But your dad's job?" I whisper.

"He works for this megacorporation. He'll find a way. It just took Mom to force him to."

She's staying. Just like that, Rachel's changing from a moveable feast to a giant immovable apple. All this symbolism, I think I like it.

CHAPTER 23

The bottom of the tub is covered with blond hair. Eric sits on the rim with his back to me as I stand in the tub on a carpet of hair. First I cut it down to a heavy stubble; now I use the razor on him.

He shivers as I massage cool mint shaving cream into his scalp. Whenever I eat anything with peppermint, I'm reminded of his smooth bald head. It's this bizarre sensual association. I turn the water on bearably hot and run the razor under it—a regular razor, not a straight razor. He doesn't trust me that much.

Eric tilts his head back and I start shaving by his right sideburn, then around behind his ear, slowly making my way across his head.

"Got another joke for you," he says, looking up at me looking down.

I groan. "Is it going to hurt?"

"Maybe." He smiles.

"Careful now. I'm holding a very sharp blade here."

I rinse stubble off under the faucet, preparing myself to be assaulted by his wit.

"So, this is one of those Zen riddles," he says. "You know, like a question without an answer. Like: 'What is the sound of one hand clapping?' "

I give him a playful slap on the cheek. "That is the sound of one hand clapping."

"Ow. Come on. Can I tell my joke?"

"Go ahead, my love."

"The question is: 'If Helen Keller falls in a forest, does she make a sound?' "

I stare at his upside-down, stupid little smile. I bend down and give him a reverse kiss, my nose to his chin, his chin to my nose.

"Shut up," I whisper into his lips.

"I don't usually let my barber do this," he says.

The shaving cream smells good enough to eat. I get some on my shirt and rub it in, knowing I'll smell my shirt when I go home and probably sleep in it.

I'm halfway done with Eric's head. His eyes are closed, his body leaning back against mine. I'm ankle-deep in hot water; all this blond hair is clogging the drain.

I tried something totally insane yesterday. Over at Rachel's place, in her closet, we took turns singing "You'll Never Know Her." She likes that song better than "Hate You," because she can relate to unrequited love. First Rachel sang it, then I gave it a try. We finally decided on me singing the main part, with her doing the chorus. I've got it on tape and it actually works with our two voices together. They sort of balance each other, her light voice and my dark one. I'm going to play the tape for Eric when we get out of the tub.

The steamy water rises ever so slowly up my legs,

reaching my calves. I'm almost done now. Just this little bit left.

The smell of mint from Eric's smooth scalp makes me want to kiss it, and give it a little cat-lick.

I'm done. Setting the razor down, I run my hands under the faucet until they're nice and hot. Then I wipe Eric's head clean. It's new, beautiful, bald and minty. I run my hands over it, brush just the ghost of a kiss behind his ear.

The water's just an inch below my knees, threatening to flood our small part of the world. I turn it off and step out of the tub onto the bath mat. Eric stands and wipes clear the steamed-up mirror so he can see.

"What do you think?" he asks. I stand beside him in the mirror. There we are. Me. Eric. Us.

"I think you're brand spanking new," I say.

I think I am too.

ABOUT THE AUTHOR

Graham McNamee grew up in Toronto and lives in Vancouver. He's a "book person" who has worked in bookstores, libraries, and a bookbinding factory. His hobbies are drawing and photography.

Hate You was chosen as the Honor Book in the Fifteenth Annual Delacorte Press Contest for a First Young Adult Novel.